DEATHLINE

Recent Titles by Jane Aiken Hodge from Severn House

A DEATH IN TWO PARTS
SUSAN IN AMERICA

DEATHLINE

Jane Aiken Hodge

This first world edition published in Great Britain 2003 by
SEVERN HOUSE PUBLISHERS LTD of
9–15 High Street, Sutton, Surrey SM1 1DF.
This first world edition published in the USA 2003 by
SEVERN HOUSE PUBLISHERS INC of
595 Madison Avenue, New York, N.Y. 10022.

British Library Cataloguing in Publication Data

Hodge, Jane Aiken, 1917-
    Deathline
    1.   Terminal care - Fiction
    2.   Female friendship - Fiction
    I.   Title
    823.9'14 [F]

    ISBN 0-7278-5998-6

Typeset by Hewer Text Ltd.,
Edinburgh, Scotland.
Printed and bound in Great Britain by
MPG Books Ltd., Bodmin, Cornwall.

In loving memory of
Beatrice Taussig and Eunice Frost

One

'**M**other left the house to Frank? I don't believe it!' Helen Westley stared at the solicitor across his outsize office desk. 'After all her promises! I won't believe it!' But her world was shaking around her.

'It's true, I'm afraid.' John Barnes shifted uneasily in his chair. 'That's why I asked you to come in. I thought you ought to know before the funeral. The will has never been changed, you see; the one she made on marriage to your father. It was a reasonable enough disposition at the time, mind you. The house to your half-brother, whose father's it had been, and the rest of her estate to her new husband.'

'But that was thirty-five years ago, when she married Father!'

'Yes.' He looked with compassion and apology across his desk at the woman who appeared, in shock, every one of her thirty-three years. 'I did try to point out to your mother, Miss Westley, that things had changed, that she ought to rethink the basic principle of the will, but you know how she was. It was all I could do to get her to make the essential alterations when your father died.'

'And she collapsed and summoned me home from college to look after her. Promised me the house when she died. Did you know that?'

'Miss Westley, I was afraid that was how it was. But what could I do? She was my client.'

And I was just a useful daughter at home, thought Helen. But she did not say it. Instead, she asked the obvious question: 'So – the rest of the estate? What, roughly, does that mean, after all those years of comfortable invalidism. I never could get her to talk about money.'

'No more could I,' he admitted. 'And you are absolutely right, of course. There have been drawings on her capital. Those cruises she used to take, before she became bed-ridden, and the extra help you had to have afterwards. It all meant capital, and I never could make her understand why her income dwindled as a result.'

'No, I don't suppose you could,' with the ghost of a sympathetic grin that reminded him how much he had always liked quiet Helen Westley, and made him feel guiltier than ever. Best get it over with. It was the kindest thing to do, for both of them. 'What I couldn't make her see –' he found it hard to meet her eyes – 'was what the soaring value of the house was going to mean in taxes when she died. Frank Dobson, your half-brother, and I are joint executors as you know, and it will take a little time to work out the figures, but I devoutly hope we shall find enough capital left to produce some kind of small income for you. It's a mercy you've got that good job, Miss Westley. You were so wise to get in carers for your mother and hang on to that.'

'Mr Barnes.' She was absolutely not going to cry. 'I was made redundant yesterday.'

'What? I don't believe it!' His turn to say that, Helen thought bleakly. 'But you've done so well there. I'd always heard you were the backbone of the place, kept it together, were irreplaceable.'

'We've been taken over. We're going hi-tech. And no one is irreplaceable, Mr Barnes. Of course I've been away a lot while Mother was dying. So: three months' pay and a glowing testimonial. And no qualifications. I went straight there, you know, not back to college, because it was local and Mother said she couldn't manage without me. It was such fun; they were starting out too, we all learned on the job. Five of us at first, sharing everything, working things out together. Everything's different now.'

'And not necessarily better.' He said it for her. 'I'm truly sorry, Miss Westley. Does your brother know?'

'Why should he? We've never been close. He's so much older, more like an uncle.' And not one she could ever like. There was so much she must not say.

'I'm seeing him again tomorrow. Forgive me, Miss Westley, I must get this clear – what are the terms of your . . .' He paused, searching for the tactful word.

'Dismissal? Three months' pay and out on my ear, there and then. The new broom's sweeping fast. I had to borrow a plastic bag to take home my bits and pieces.' Not home any more. Her brother's house. Helen's nails dug deep into the palms of her hands as she answered the next question. 'No, no pension. It wasn't that kind of operation.'

'I suppose not. Three months' pay is hardly generous. Perhaps we should fight it, try to get you a little more—'

'No. Thanks, but no. Waste of time and money. What's done's done. And I mustn't take up any more of your time, Mr Barnes.' She picked up her bag from the floor, and made to rise.

'Just a minute.' He had read her mind. 'I'm not charging you for this meeting, Miss Westley, don't think so for a moment. And I must have the position clear so I can put it to your brother. He has to know how you are placed.' He had seen her instant reaction. 'What your plans are?' He made it a question.

'Plans?' She looked at him bleakly. 'They were based on the house, of course. I hadn't decided whether to sell it and use the proceeds to get some training, or whether I could stay in it and make it support me somehow. Rent rooms or something. I loved that house.' They both noticed the past tense. 'Well, I've lived there all my life.' She stood up. 'Now I just have to start thinking all over again. You've been very kind, Mr Barnes, and I thank you for it. You'll let me know, as soon as you can, just how small the estate is going to be, won't you? You can see it is going to have bearing. And –' it had only just struck her – 'ask my brother how long I can stay in the house, please? That will have bearing too.' Something in the quality of his silence alerted her. 'He's said something about that already?'

'I know he means to sell,' he told her. 'With vacant possession and as soon as possible. He's a little overextended in the city himself, needs the capital. But of course nothing happens at once after a death. It will take longer than your three months—'

'Will he charge me rent, do you think? I wouldn't put it past him for a minute. Ought I to make a list of things I own in that house, Mr Barnes?'

'He did mention an inventory. Best to keep everything businesslike, even when it's in the family.'

'Family?' She looked at her watch. 'I must go. I wouldn't want to be late for the funeral. It was good of you to fit me in. I did need to know. Before I meet them.'

'That's what I thought. And I'm sorry about the funeral, too, Miss Westley. Frank Dobson insisted on Putney Vale and a cremation, the cheapest option. I told him your mother wanted to be buried in the graveyard, beside your father, but I'm afraid he dismissed that as old lady's nonsense.'

'I'm sure he did. And Mother really enjoyed planning her funeral. And the wake, back at the house, afterwards. Oh!' Suddenly she understood. Even Frank had blanched at the thought of entertaining the mourners in the house that was to be his, should have been hers. She rather thought that Mr Barnes had come to the same conclusion. 'Oh well,' standing up. 'At least Mother had fun planning it. He can't take that away. I do thank you for being so kind, Mr Barnes.'

'I wish I could do more, but I promise you, I'll do my best. How are you going to get to Putney Vale? It's an awkward place without a car.' They were both remembering that Helen's mother had sold the car when she became bedridden.

'I've a taxi picking me up from here. It's about due. Frank said he'd bring me back.' She was glad now that she had decided not to try and get back to the house first. She needed time before she faced it with the knowledge that it was not hers.

'I feel guilty, not coming.' He was showing her down the stairs.

'Don't. It's not the funeral Mother wanted. I don't think she will be there, somehow.' She thought of her father's funeral service, held in the church across the garden from the house, with all the neighbours crowding in to say goodbye to a good friend, and the choir singing for nothing because he had been such a faithful supporter. 'And nor will anyone else,' she told the solicitor, returning his firm handshake at the street door and noting with relief that her taxi was there, waiting.

'No, I am afraid not. It's not easy by public transport. I shall be thinking of you, Miss Westley.'

And she thought, getting into the cab, that he really would.

The traffic on the Upper Richmond Road was worse than usual, and she was too busy worrying about being late to think much about the shock she had just received. Her only thought was that she must not let it show; she must carry it off, whatever happened. She had been angry, but was glad now, that Frank had made no arrangement for the wake their mother had wanted.

'There you are, love, just made it.' The friendly taxi driver swooped to a halt and she paid him quickly, tipped him well, and followed the small group who were just going into the glum little chapel, finding herself, with relief, next to her niece Jan in the front pew. Beyond her, Marika Dobson was kneeling in token prayer, immensely elegant, as always, in fashionable charcoal grey. And beyond her again Frank leaned forward to give Helen a glance both relieved and reproving. But the piped music had changed; the service was starting.

How Mother would have hated it. Standing and sitting as required, joining in the one last, ill-sung, ill-chosen hymn, Helen wondered why she should mind this after what her mother had done to her, but she did. The minister, speaking briefly about the dear departed, called her Wesley, not Westley, and Helen felt Jan's hand close firm and warm on her own. She went on holding it until the curtains drew mercifully together and they began the awkward shuffle into the grey afternoon where the next party was waiting.

'Party is hardly the word.' Helen was surprised to realize that she had said this aloud to Jan, still close beside her, while her parents spoke their thanks to the clergyman.

'No.' Jan understood. 'I'm sorry about the wake, Helen, but maybe . . .'

'It's best this way,' Helen confirmed, as her brother turned to include the two of them in the little group around the clergyman.

'My sister.' He introduced them. 'And my daughter.'

'My deepest sympathy, Miss Wesley.' His hand was moist.

'The name is Westley.' She looked full at him for a moment, then turned away, unable to bear his stammered apology.

'You might have spared us that.' Frank had helped his wife carefully into the front of the BMW, now opened the back door for Helen.

'Yes, a pity. He made me too cross. Poor young man. I was sorry the minute I'd said it. Just drop me at the Sheen Lane lights, Frank. No need to struggle down to the house.'

'Right. Seat belt, Jan.' Did he have eyes in the back of his head? 'Hideous time of day for a funeral, but it was the only slot I could get.' He was now driving very fast indeed across Richmond Park. 'Sorry to have to rush you, Helen, but Marika has this charity do at the Hurlingham Club. She's one of the lady patronesses. Mustn't be late. And Jan's got a load of work this vac. Burning the midnight oil like mad, aren't we, Jan? And back to the old grind for me. No peace for the wicked financier.' He slowed just a little as they reached the Sheen Gate. 'And the traffic's going to be hell, this time of the evening, so if you really don't mind being dropped off at the lights.' He blasted his horn at a pedestrian who showed signs of stepping off the kerb. 'You'll let me know if I can do anything to help with the move, won't you, Helen? Sooner the better, don't you think? Get it over with, you know? It's always easier to sell with vacant possession. And empty, of course. You must make me a

list of what you would like to take. Anything within reason.
I know Mother would have wanted that. This do you?'

'Yes, thanks.' Jan had her hand again, trying to tell her
something. Helen leaned towards her niece and kissed her
suddenly, warmly, for the first time ever. 'Goodbye, Jan.
Thanks for the lift, Frank. Bye, Marika.' She was safe on
the pavement, shaking in every limb.

She crossed twice on the green man, waiting for it
dutifully as she seldom did, then wove her way like an
automaton along the crowded pavement to where Church
Path turned off illogically across later developments to take
her to the church near the river and the house that was not
hers. It sat cornerwise from the church, isolated in its tiny
patch of garden, a high wall with no gate separating this
from the graveyard. The entrance was on the other side of
the house and when she reached it, she paused. When she
had left it this morning she had been full of plans, for the
house and for herself. Now there was nothing.

Frank had managed to make it brutally clear that he
wanted her out as soon as possible. She ought to go in, start
thinking, packing, organizing. But instead she just stood
there, key in hand. Not yet. Too soon to face the house that
was not hers. First she needed a quick walk by the river to
clear her head and take away the taste of that sad little
service. To set about trying to forgive her mother and
replan her life.

She turned away from the house that held all of her past
and none of her future and walked briskly through the
graveyard to the path leading across the Lower Richmond
Road to the river. But when she climbed the steps over the
embankment wall to the towpath where she usually walked
she saw floodwater lapping close below on the other side,
the path itself under water. She had reckoned without the

8

moon and the tide. No walk here today. She looked quickly around. The cars on the road behind her had their lights on against the December dusk. The wind blew cooler, ruffling dark water; lights shone out on the opposite bank. In this quiet corner by the river there was nobody else in sight. An immense temptation seized her. How easy it would be. Just walk in, slip a little, stumble a little, forget you can swim, let go. All over so easily. No more planning. Just done. Done with. She was shaking again, why? Absurd. It would be an end to shaking. An end to everything. Cowardly? Of course. But who would mind? Mr Barnes might mind a little. And so would Jan. How odd. She was remembering that firm, warm, hand, the quick, impulsive kiss. If she walked into the river now, Jan would think it her father's fault.

She turned away from the tempting water, returned to the road and stood for a moment hesitating, gazing at the traffic, heavier now, the rush hour in full swing. She was still not ready to go back to the empty house. The towpath upriver by the bridge would be above water, she knew, but it was almost dark. Stupid to get herself mugged by walking there, alone, in her funeral clothes, with all her bank cards in her bag. She started upriver just the same, passed the brewery, then turned on impulse back into town. That mad moment by the river had shaken things loose in her mind, a great kaleidoscopic shift had taken place and she knew what she had to do. Get away. At once. How?

She reached the small municipal green patch by the railway line and sat for a moment on a bench, shivering a little with returning life, to reckon expedients. What could she do? Where could she go? There was no one she could invite herself to stay with, particularly now, just before Christmas, when everyone had their own family commitments. Hotels would be booked solid at this time of year, and full of pseudo-merriment. Besides, she could not afford one. It would be crazy to start spending her savings on their high Christmas rates at this time of crisis.

Crisis. The word threw up a picture of her mother, many years ago, before she became bedridden, sitting on the sofa and telling a caller that in a crisis she always relied on *The Lady*. 'Always have, always will, and that magazine has never let me down. Furnished houses, holidays, help in the hour of need,' she used to say. And it had been true. Helen got up from the bench and turned, with purpose now, to the level crossing by the station. At the newsagent in Sheen Lane she found that *The Lady* had changed, become glossy, since she had last seen it, but it still had a reassuring number of pages of small ads. She bought it and headed for home, wishing absurdly that she had managed to persuade her mother to let her have a cat. But Mother had been afraid of tripping over it. Poor Mother had been afraid of so many things, had given up so easily, dwindling into inaction, into one ailment after another, and so to dusty death.

'And you're a fine one to talk!' Had she said it aloud? Someone on the pavement by the traffic lights had given her an odd look. She turned down the path that led to what had been home, savaging herself for cowardice. Because she had tried, or because she had failed? She had so nearly done it. She was actually blushing with shame and anger as she turned the key in the lock and threw open the front door of her brother's house. It looked just the same. How odd. She dumped her bag, threw off her coat, turned on the gas fire, poured herself a glass of sherry and opened *The Lady* at the Situations Vacant column. What a lot of need: flexinannies; friendly au pairs; mother's helps. But what am I?

It jumped out of the column at her:

Angry old woman with house seeks companion, with some money.

And a telephone number. Not London. How rash, she thought, to print that, reached for the phone and dialled.

The phone rang for a very long time and she was just thinking of hanging up, when there was a kind of clatter at the other end of the line and a shaky voice asked, 'Is that Dr Braddock?'

'No, I'm afraid not,' Helen said. 'It's about your advertisement in *The Lady*.'

'Oh, that. I'd quite given up hope. When can you come?'

'But you don't know anything about me!'

'I know I need you, don't I? Nobody's come for a week now. That's why I want Dr Braddock. There's no milk and no eggs and no bread. And the heating's gone mad. He said I mustn't try and go downstairs on my own, that's why I was trying to get him. I can't just lie here in bed and freeze to death, can I?'

'How old are you?'

'Sensible question. Eighty. Fine till I got these aches, had this fall, got old. Never thought I'd see it. Never thought I'd say it. How old are you?'

'Thirty-three. My name's Helen Westley. My mother just died. I've got to get out of the house. But I've not got a lot of money, I'm afraid. I've got some redundancy pay and some savings and a little coming from the estate.'

'When the lawyers get done with it. How soon can you get here?'

'Where's "here"?'

'Another good question. Leyning, near Lewes, East Sussex.' The thin old voice was beginning to fail. 'Beatrice

11

Tresikker, the High House, Leyning. Taxi from the station. I'll pay. Key's in the flowerpot.'

'But that's not safe!'

'Nothing's safe. I've got to crawl to the loo now. See you in the morning, Helen Westley.'

'Can you manage for tonight?'

'I've managed for a week, haven't I?' Helen heard a clunk as the receiver was dropped back into its base.

Quite crazy. She sat staring at the silent phone. What in the world had she committed herself to? Call back after a suitable interval and say it was impossible? No, *that* was impossible. She could not leave that frail-sounding eighty-year-old all by herself in a house with no bread and no milk and no eggs and the heating gone mad. There had been a spirit she had liked in that dwindling voice, and Beatrice Tresikker's description of her plight had been both terse and lucid. Why angry old woman? she wondered, finished her sherry and began to plan.

Two

H elen's first decision was easily arrived at. She would tell no one what she was doing until she had seen Beatrice Tresikker and found out how the land lay. Whatever happened, she would stock the house up, see the old lady through Christmas and the looming millennium. Then it would be time enough for the two of them to think about the future. At least her own immediate problem had been solved: she had board and useful occupation for Christmas and New Year's after all. She went upstairs and packed a holiday ration of warm clothes into a small case from the elegant, expensive lightweight set her mother had bought during her cruising days. The rest of her clothes went easily into her mother's other cases, to be left in her bedroom along with her other effects, ruthlessly collected from all over the house. If she decided to stay with Beatrice Tresikker (Mrs or Miss?) Brother Frank could have them sent on to her.

In the morning, her conscience pricking her, she rang the one neighbour with whom her mother had remained on good terms. Miss Jepson was full of apologies for missing the funeral and thought Helen very sensible to get away to the country for Christmas and 'that dreadful millennium'. Of course she would keep a neighbourly eye on the house, but should Helen not tell the police? Helen supposed she should, and when she had battled her way through the minefield of their switchboard left Beatrice Tresikker's name, address and telephone number with them, though they did not seem much interested. She had managed to get through to rail enquiries too, and set off at last without a backward glance, to catch the connection for the Leyning train at Clapham Junction. Pausing at the newsagent to cancel her mother's *Telegraph* she bought herself *The Independent* and agreed that she was lucky to be getting away so early for Christmas. It would be mayhem by the end of the week, the girl said.

Could it be only Tuesday? She seemed to have lived several lifetimes since Monday morning. Death times? But here was Clapham Junction and she must hurry across the spreading station to catch her train. The sooner she got to the High House in Leyning where Beatrice Tresikker awaited her, the better. She did not like the thought of the aches and the fall, though some sign of old age at eighty was hardly surprising. She sat gazing out of the carriage window at rows of suburban houses, *The Independent* neglected on her lap, and wondered what the angry old woman would be like. Had there been a trace of an accent behind the standard vowels of that dwindling voice? She rather thought there had but could not identify it.

It had been a murky morning, but presently the train pulled out of a long tunnel into sunshine and more green fields than houses. How long since she had last got out of London? Hard to remember. After her mother had taken to her bed it had become increasingly difficult to leave her, even for a weekend. Too many planned visits to friends had had to be cancelled at the last minute because Mother had had one of her attacks, or taken against the carer. In the end, friends had stopped inviting her, particularly as the return visits she had tried to arrange to the theatre or concerts were just as liable to last-minute sabotage. If I do decide to stay with Beatrice Tresikker – if she wants me, she reminded herself – I must make sure that we lay down the ground rules clearly from the start. Useful to be so well versed in the caring business.

After Gatwick, the country got better and better, with woods instead of fields, and a viaduct with views that took her breath away. Turning from side to side, not to miss a thing, she was aware of a strange sensation. She seemed to be enjoying herself, and felt grateful to the unknown Beatrice Tresikker. The train divided at Haywards Heath, but the guard who checked her ticket had reassured her that she was in the right bit, and that Leyning was the stop after next. And now she saw the long line of the south downs, their folds and hollows thrown into relief by sun and shadow. Whatever happened when she got to the High House, she was glad she had come. If this turned out to be a wild goose chase, maybe to a madwoman, which was entirely possible, she would find a bed and breakfast place and spend the night in Leyning just the same. They were running through what must be its outskirts now, and she liked what she saw, as suburban fringe gave way to a great slope of graveyard with a church above, while on the other side a huddle of red brick houses clung to another hill as if they had been there for ever.

There really was a taxi in the station yard, and her slight anxiety about the sparse address was relieved at once when the elderly driver, who had actually got out of his cab to take her case, opened the front door for her and said, 'High House, is it? Fancy that. How is old Madam Tresikker? I haven't driven her for . . . can't think how long. Good to hear she's still alive.' He closed the door on her.

'That's a relief,' she said as he got in and started the car. 'I was afraid the address might not be enough.'

'Oh, we all know the High House,' he told her cheerfully. 'And Madam Tresikker. A good tipper. Not lavish, you know, but fair. Understands about waiting time, too. Not like some. Mind you, if you were late, she were poison. No tip then. But, hey, you're not a relative are you? A lost niece or something? I reckon she could do with one of those.'

'No, no kin, and I've never met her.' They were driving past Safeway and it reminded her of something. 'Is there a local shop anywhere handy where I could drop off for a minute and get a few supplies? She said on the phone that she was out of everything.'

'You spoke up just in time.' He swung the car into a side street. 'Mr Patel will see you right. He stocks just about everything, I reckon. Pricey, mind you, but much quicker than Safeway except when school's just out. There'll be waiting time, of course,' he warned, stopping the cab outside a little shop with a window full of advertisements.

The grey-haired man at the till gave her a beaming smile as she picked up a basket and quickly collected eggs, bread, milk, butter, tomatoes, sliced ham, orange juice, a can of condensed soup and some bacon. Reaching the checkout, she saw a small wine section and added a bottle of her favourite dry sherry. It reminded her of something else. 'Coffee?' she asked, putting her basket on the counter.

'Round there,' he pointed and began to ring up her purchases. 'Taxi waiting?'

'Yes.' On an impulse, because she liked him, she added, 'I'm going to the High House. Do you know it?'

'Old Madam Tresikker? Sure do. And glad to hear it too. Haven't heard from her for a while; thought she might be dead. Except we'd have heard about that all right, lady like her. Ill, is she?'

'She doesn't sound too good. I'm on my way to see. Is it far from here? Will I be able to walk it?'

'Course. Active lady like you. Ten minutes, fifteen maybe. Quicker on foot by the lanes.' He was packing her groceries efficiently into two bags. 'But I'll deliver if you phone. Always used to. Charge, of course. After hours. Here.' He handed her a printed sheet, took her money, gave her the change and came out from behind the counter to open the door for her.

'Thank you. You're very kind.'

He beamed at her. 'Thank you, ma'am. Look forward to seeing you, and I hope you find the old lady OK.'

'What a nice man,' she said to the driver. 'Thank you for taking me to him. Where's he from?' She expected him to say Pakistan or India, but he surprised her. 'Bradford. Born there, didn't like it much. Came down here five, six years ago. Bit of a hard time at first. Well, I expect you can imagine. Leyning's not a bad place, but it's got its yobs like everywhere.' He was driving slowly over a narrow old brick bridge. 'That's the Ley,' he told her. 'Runs into the Ouse a few miles out of town. Now you're in Old Leyning. There was an abbey at the top of the hill; the church is all that's left of it. Madam Tresikker told me her house was built of abbey stone. She loves that house, talked about it a lot. Told me once it saved her life. I don't know what she meant. It's not where I'd want my old mum to be living.' He turned the car sharply uphill and round a couple of hairpin bends, then pulled up in front of a flight of stone steps. 'There,' he said. 'See what I mean?'

Helen got out and stood looking up the steps to the house above them; two storeys of grey stone like the steps, with a built-on porch for the front door, big sash windows along the front and an extraordinary turret at one end. 'Goodness gracious,' she said and then, 'Oh, thank you, how kind,' as the driver got her case out of the boot and carried it up the steps. 'And how much?' she asked, putting her groceries down and hoping she would get the tip just right, like Madam Tresikker. Paying him, she faced another problem: which flowerpot held the key? Twin bay trees stood on either side of the porch and pots of geraniums, some still in straggling bloom, lined the terrace.

'Thank you, miss.' The tip had been right. He smiled at her. 'It's usually in one of the bay tree pots,' he told her.

'You mean everyone knows?' Appalled. 'But it's not safe!'

'Well, yes and no. Most people know about the key, but most people know she's nothing left to steal. She's been done one, two, three times, standing alone like this. "All my pretty ones", she told me once. Nothing's left but a lot of old books, and who wants those? Best of luck, miss.' He produced a card and handed it to her. 'Here's our number when you need us, but the old lady knows it. If she remembers it.' And on that slightly daunting note he left her standing there, got into the cab and drove away.

No time now for the view the house commanded. Somewhere inside the old lady had presumably heard the car, would be waiting for her. She found the key tucked down at the back of the right-hand bay tree and was glad to see that at least it was a Chubb. Turning it with some difficulty she opened the door and stepped into a tiled hall that ran from front to back of the house. 'It's Helen Westley.' Her voice sounded strange to her. 'I'm here.'

No answer. She locked the door behind her, picked up a pile of what looked like junk mail and stood looking around. Open doors to the right and left showed a sitting room and dining room, scantily furnished, deeply dusty, very empty. Built-in bookshelves from floor to ceiling lined each side of the hall, crammed almost beyond bursting with books. Nobody on this floor. And where were the stairs?

She found them behind one of two doors that faced each other at the far end of the hall. What a strange house. 'It's Helen Westley,' she called again as she started upstairs. 'Are you up there?' Still no answer. Deeply anxious now, she hurried up the awkwardly turning stair and emerged in another long hall. And now she did think she heard the faintest of sounds from the front of the house. 'I'm coming.' She pushed gently on a half-open door and stood for a moment gazing at chaos. Time for that later. Her concern was for the figure slumped in the big bed. All she could see was short, shaggy white hair. 'Are you all right, Ms Tresikker?'

'Mrs. No.' It was a thread of a voice. 'Doctor said drink . . . Can't . . .' An empty jug on the bedside table made the point for her. If she had been crawling to the loo there was no way she could have fetched herself water.

Filling the jug in the en suite bathroom, Helen looked about her at more chaos. Clean chaos, she noted with relief, the loo had been flushed and the room was dusty, not dirty.

'Let me help you sit up.' She put an experienced arm round Mrs Tresikker, pulling up pillows with the other hand. Then she held the glass to dry lips that drank desperately.

'Thanks,' said the old lady at last. 'You know how.'

'Yes.' Helen put down the glass and they looked at each other. Beatrice Tresikker was brown and wiry like an old root that has been exposed to wind and sun for years. Her short, white hair stood up on end; she was wearing a brilliant peacock-blue bedjacket and leaned back against dark purple pillows that matched the duvet cover.

The old lady was seeing a woman beyond her first youth, wearing a navy-blue all-purpose coat, which she now took off and laid on a chair, revealing a business-like navy suit. Taking off the suit jacket and rolling up emerald-green sleeves, Helen made a final adjustment to the supporting pillows, drew up a chair beside the bed, sat down on it and smiled. 'What first?' she asked. 'Are you hungry too? I brought some food.' And, as an afterthought, 'And a bottle of dry sherry.'

'Fetch it then,' said Beatrice Tresikker. 'Glasses in the kitchen. You'll find them. Restful.'

'I won't be long.'

'No hurry. I'll wait. Been living on bananas. You might take the skins down.' A gesture drew Helen's attention to a waste basket on the far side of the bed which proved to be full of banana skins, explaining a curious over-sweet smell that permeated the room. 'The last one this morning. Glad you came, but not starving. Yet. Wondering a bit.'

'I should think you might be.' Helen picked up the waste basket. 'Anything else to go?' She glanced round the room, spotted a plate and glass on the floor by the bed and picked them up. 'I'll be right back.'

'Don't rush. We've time. Don't be shocked, either. God knows what it's like downstairs. Wendy's good as gold but she only comes once a week. I can't afford more and she's not got the time anyway. Single mum,' she said, as if that explained everything.

'When does she come?' Helen paused in the doorway.

'Thursday. Ten till twelve. She got me the bananas.'

'And you've seen no one since?' Appalled. 'What are the social services doing?'

'It's a long story. Better over sherry?'

'Right.' She was relieved to find that the kitchen was comparatively clean. Single mother Wendy obviously had her priorities right. It was a pleasant room with a window over the sink that looked across a rising slope of shaggy garden to a high stone wall. Cupboards to right and left above the sink held china on one side and glass on the other – odd pieces of good glass; the old Wedgwood celadon Helen remembered from childhood. Heavy Le Creuset saucepans in another cupboard suggested a real cook. How strange to try and read a woman from her kitchen. There was a small deep freeze with a microwave on top, and a real larder with nothing in it but some ancient looking tins, amongst which Helen was delighted to find one of stuffed green olives. She had been worrying a little about sherry on a stomach that had met nothing but bananas for the last five days. How many bananas? she wondered, finding a light tray in a cupboard. A tin opener proved more elusive, but she found it at last at the back of a drawer and drained the olives into a little dish someone had bought in Avignon.

Back upstairs, she found Beatrice Tresikker sitting very upright in bed, looking anxious. 'Loo first, please. Do you mind?' she said. 'Nicer than crawling.'

'Course I don't mind. I've been helping my mother for years. Dressing gown?'

'No need.' She was light as a feather, Helen found, and much easier to help than her solid mother had been. Placed safely on the seat, she dismissed Helen. 'Call when I'm ready. Shut the door. Thanks.' The word seemed to surprise her.

Now Helen had time to look round the shambles of a room. Great piles of clothes on all the furniture, and books

21

everywhere: piles on the floor by the bed, piles on the dressing table by the window; paperbacks, hardbacks, two unmistakable London Library books, many of them with markers in or their dust jackets tucked in to mark a place. And a pile of folders on the beside table, and on the floor, full of handwritten notes.

The violent ringing of a bell made her start. The front door. 'Are you all right for a minute?' she called through the bathroom door. 'I'll see who it is.'

'Do,' came a croak. 'Taking my time. No hurry.'

As she negotiated the awkward stairs the doorbell rang again, louder than ever, making her suddenly furious. She turned the key in the lock, flung it open and confronted a tall man in a baggy grey tweed suit, bag in hand. 'You must be the doctor,' she said and, simultaneously, 'Who the hell are you?' he asked, stepping across the threshold.

'Helen Westley. I answered an advertisement.' She found herself moving aside to let him pass. 'Lucky thing I did; she'd been on her own for five days. What on earth are your social services doing down here?' And then, as he headed down the hall for the stairs, 'Hang on, she's in the loo.'

'Oh.' This did stop him momentarily in his tracks. 'How long have you been here?' He was looking at the suitcase and grocery bags she had dumped in the hall.

'Fifteen minutes? Long enough to be glad I got here when I did. She's been living on bananas since her cleaner came last week.'

'Then we'd better not stay gossiping here but get her out of the loo so I can check her over.'

There was nothing for it but to follow him as he headed up the stairs, bag in hand, calling as he went, 'Mrs Tresikker, it's Hugh Braddock.'

Ten minutes later, he closed his bag. 'You're a survivor, that's all: like it or not, Beatrice Tresikker. I'll see myself out, Miss Wesley, and drop the key back through the letter box. I'm sorry if I startled you.' He had been aware of her simmering irritation. 'I thought you were burglars.'

'Oh.' She had not thought of this and it made her crosser than ever. 'But what about treatment? What do I do?'

'Bed rest. The pills for pain as before. She knows. And you seem to know the ropes.'

She thought it grudgingly said, and followed him to the stairhead to ask, 'And when will you come again?'

'No need. She'll mend. She's a great mender, Mrs Tresikker. It's not a broken hip, just a chipped bone. Nothing to be done but bear it. And now if you'll excuse me, Miss Wesley, I've a partner down with flu and ten more patients to see before surgery.'

'Westley,' she said, but he was running down the stairs and did not hear, or at least did not answer.

'What a rude man.' She returned to the bedroom as the front door slammed below.

'Yes, isn't he? In the good old days we'd have given him a glass of sherry. They are gone for ever, so let's just have it ourselves.' But she looked much better, Helen noticed, for the doctor's brusque ministrations.

'The trouble is, I lose my temper,' said the old lady surprisingly as Helen poured sherry. 'Can't stand stupidity, never could. Braddock may be rude, but he's not stupid. But those carers he sent in. Well! And I won't be called "love" either. So they didn't come back.'

'So what do I call you? If I'm going to stay.'

'I hope you are. You're not stupid either. Anyone can see that. Having a crisis or something? Yes?'

'Yes. It would suit me very well to stay. At least over

23

Christmas and the millennium. Get you stocked up and sorted out, and then we can think about it?'

'Fine with me.' Beatrice Tresikker had drunk half her sherry and looked mildly pinker. 'It's a funny thing,' she said thoughtfully. 'These last months that I've been stuck in the house because of this wretched pain, I've thought I wanted to die. Told Braddock so, but he wouldn't help – said he can't, plague take him. But do you know, when I was lying here all weekend trying to work out how to fill the water jug, I found I want to live. Things to do. Well, there's the book.' Her eyes moved to the table covered in folders. 'Can you type?'

'Yes. What's the book?'

'I call it *A Final Account*. One I've got to settle. With myself as much as anything. The name Tresikker mean anything to you?'

'No. Should it?'

'I think so. He was a poet. Before the war. Good, he was. But he . . . what did he do? Wasted it, lost it, they swept him under the carpet. It's a long story.' She was beginning to slump down among the pillows.

'We need our lunch,' said Helen. 'Soup and toast do you?'

Three

By tacit consent, they ate separately, Helen downstairs at the kitchen table with her still unread *Independent*. 'You look worn out,' she said, upstairs again to fetch the tray. 'Let me settle you for a nap. Loo first?'

'Please.' They had worked out a technique and it was easier this time.

While her patient was immured, Helen gave the bed a shake and promised it clean sheets in the morning. She must find the airing cupboard, get her bearings generally. Helping Beatrice Tresikker back from the bathroom, she showed her a little old-fashioned hand bell she had found in a kitchen cupboard. 'I'm going to unpack and have a bit of a tidy,' she said. 'I'll shut your door so I don't disturb you; just ring that if you need me. Easier than shouting.'

'You think of everything,' said Beatrice Tresikker. 'I'm not much of a hostess, I'm afraid, but at least the spare bed's made up. Be sure and find everything you need, only please don't . . .' Her eyes were beginning to close. She jerked herself awake. 'What was I saying?'

'Something you don't want me to do.' Helen had noticed that the old lady sometimes started a sentence and lost her way in it, and had promised herself that she would have a word with Dr Braddock about this, if he ever came back.

'Can't remember. Don't work too hard, I expect. You

25

look tired . . . Been having a hard time, haven't you? Get a rest . . .' Her eyes were closing again.

Helen put the tray on the table in the hall and shut the bedroom door gently behind her. She paused for a minute, tempted to explore at once, but habit was too strong for her and she took the tray down, stacked the dishes and armed herself with the cleanest duster from the big cupboard beside the larder.

It was rather daunting to find the closet in the front spare room full of Mrs Tresikker's ancient evening wear, purple and crimson and dull gold, all smelling mustily of old, old scent. Surely somewhere in the house there must be an empty cupboard where these could hang until she persuaded the old lady to give them away? But the closet in the bedroom behind Mrs Tresikker's turned out to hold what looked like several generations of cotton dresses in muted greys and mauves and dusky pinks, also smelling faintly of perfumes long ago.

Hopefully opening another door at the end of the hall, Helen found a spiral stair, and remembered that extraordinary turret. It must be up above the extension that housed the larder, broom cupboard and downstairs lavatory. She felt like someone out of *The Arabian Nights* as she climbed the twisting stairs, which were far dustier than anything she had seen so far.

And at the top, what a room. It seemed to consist entirely of windows and bookcases. A wide divan bed under the left-hand window was heaped with brilliant cushions; a leather-topped desk covered in books commanded the view from the central window, while a low mahogany chest of drawers stood in front of the third. A curtained recess beside the door provided the only hanging space, and it was bulging with a man's clothes, explaining, she thought, the faint suggestion of cigarettes that hung about the room. The air was dead in here, as if it had not been opened up for years. She moved instinctively to throw up the sash of the big central window, then stood there, dumbstruck, gazing at the view. This was why the turret had been built. The extra feet of height gave the windows clearance above the line of hills beyond the town, over fields and woods to a distant silver line that must be the sea.

This was Mr Tresikker's room, of course, the poet who had been swept under the carpet. What an odd phrase to use of one's husband. And what had happened to him? The books on the desk were almost all of poetry: Eliot and Yeats, Byron and Shelley and Keats; a battered old *Oxford Book of Metaphysical Verse*. Nothing, so far as she could see, by Tresikker. But on the centre of the desk lay a folder with the initials P. T. ornately inscribed in old-fashioned pen and ink. She must not open it. She knew now that she ought not to be here. This was a shrine, not a room, and she was doing just what Beatrice Tresikker had started to forbid. It was obvious now that no one had been up here since the old lady had become bedridden. How long ago? Anyway, short of a total clear out, there was nowhere here to hang anything. She would just have to manage in her own room as best she could. Lucky she had brought so little.

The window must not have been open for years. It was a struggle to close it again and when she finally succeeded, it went down with an eldritch shriek that startled the quiet house. Hurrying guiltily back down the spiral stair she was sorry but not surprised to hear Mrs Tresikker's bell violently ringing. Opening the bedroom door, she saw the old lady sitting bolt upright in bed, shaking and scarlet with rage.

'I told you not to! Bloody nosy parker!' And then a stream of language, much of which Helen did not even try to understand. 'Get out!' she shouted at last. 'Go to hell and don't come back!'

'I'm sorry.' It sounded hopelessly inadequate. 'But you didn't tell me not to, you know. I think perhaps you started to and then forgot what you were going to say.'

'Blame it on me, would you? Pretend I'm off my head? Bloody, sanctimonious, interfering . . .' and another string of expletives that Helen tried not to hear. Her first instinct was to turn and run, leaving the old lady alone to simmer down, but she did not dare risk it. If Beatrice Tresikker were to work herself up to a stroke she would never forgive herself. She stood there silently and let it wash over her then, when the old woman paused at last for breath, she said, quite quietly, 'Please stop. I've said I'm sorry. I really didn't know. I won't do it again. And you're doing yourself harm.'

'Why not, if I like?' asked Beatrice Tresikker, suddenly reasonable. 'I've been wanting to die, ever since I've been so helpless, so hurting, but nobody would help. Bloody pro-life do-gooders. Are you one of them?'

'I don't know,' Helen said slowly. 'I haven't thought about it much.' Which was not true. She remembered that moment by the dark Thames, only yesterday. And there had been times, too, when she thought that if her mother had asked her to, she might have helped her find a way out of the life that she found entirely wretched.

'Well, think now,' said Beatrice Tresikker. 'Because that's part of any deal, any arrangement you and I might make. If you're still prepared to, after finding out what an old harridan I am.'

Somewhere between boast and apology, it was not quite

a question, but Helen chose to answer it. 'Oh, don't worry about that,' she said. 'As soon as I saw the room I knew I ought not to be there. I really am sorry.' So many questions. Which did she dare ask? 'Was it long ago?' she ventured.

'That he left me? Years and endless years. For a long time he came and went, called me his lodestar, his heart's centre, said he must go away but would always come back. And he loved the house, that room, that view, he could write there. I kept it always ready for him. When things didn't work out for him, he came back to me, and I comforted him. But he had to follow his muse. He sent me postcards – from Spain, from Mexico, from India . . . He was writing a philosophical epic; he used to scribble a few lines on the postcards. I've got them all, of course. And then they stopped coming. He stopped coming . . . It took me a while to realize. But if he'd died, I'd have heard, surely?'

How to put the question tactfully? Helen took the plunge. 'Had he published much? I have to admit that I don't know the name.'

'Before your time . . . He was older than me, had a great success in the thirties, when he came down from Cambridge . . . Lots of good friends . . . Older, mostly . . . The Woolfs took him under their wing a bit . . . He had poems in all the right places, but no collection . . . Everybody loved him . . . He made you feel you were the most important person in the world . . . And then the war came, everything changed, and afterwards they all turned against him, ganged up on him. Writers can be very cruel to each other . . . red in tooth and claw . . .' She was dwindling off into sleep, worn out by her fit of rage. Helen pulled the duvet up around her shoulders and crept out of the room to unpack, wondering a great deal about the vanished poet.

It was getting dark already. Too late now to go and check out the shops, and besides, she did not much like the idea of leaving Beatrice Tresikker alone after that outburst. Instead, she went downstairs and applied her mind to the kitchen, and lists. The house really was out of everything, and she wished passionately that she had a car. Even with taxis, she was going to be hard pushed to get things under control before Christmas. Especially as she really did not wish to leave Beatrice Tresikker alone for long. The bell, tinkled rather feebly this time, confirmed this instinct.

'You've not gone?' Beatrice Tresikker greeted her. 'I was afraid you might have.'

'Of course I haven't! I bet you need the loo.'

'Yes, please.'

There is something very friendly about helping and being helped. 'I was foul,' said Beatrice, back in bed. 'I'm sorry. It gets to be too much for me, sometimes, all the misery, and no one to talk to. And then I get someone, and look what I do! It would have served me right if you'd gone.'

'But I'm staying,' said Helen. 'Do you fancy a glass of sherry now, and then early supper and bed?'

'I certainly do. I seem to want to sleep all the time.'

'It's what you need, I'm sure.' And to talk, she thought, pouring the sherry. 'Tell me more about your husband. How did you meet him?'

'So long ago.' She reached out a shaking hand for her glass. 'He came on a lecture tour when I was at Vassar. Well, poetry reading, really. He read the first bits of his epic. I thought it was tremendous.' She stopped, gazing back at that vanished past.

'Vassar! You're American?' It explained that faint hint of an accent.

'Was American. I gave it up when I married Paul. When the war broke out. We were down here by then. I'd bought this house to give him some space, and be near the Woolfs. He loved giving parties, poetry readings, getting people together. And he could write in the turret room. It was perfect. No need to be married – Paul said it was old fashioned, barbaric. But then the war broke out and the embassy started badgering me, telling me to go home, so we solved the problem by nipping off to the registrar and making me British. It worked then. Citizenship at a stroke. Such a happy day; the Woolfs were our witnesses. And then it all went wrong.'

'Why?'

'Paul said he couldn't fight, have any part in the war. Said it wasn't a poet's job. He stuck to it, too, through thick and thin. The authorities gave him a hard time. Harder, I always thought, because his friends had shot off to the States. Auden and Isherwood, comfortable as you please.'

'I'm surprised you two didn't go too. With your family there?' She made it a question.

'Family! We'd had enough of them. All my family had was money. No love. A great barn of a mansion on the upper Hudson River. Van Guelder, father was, a diamond family from Amsterdam, went to the States and got richer. Mother was from South Carolina, hated the whole business. Bored to tears up there, and when she had us twins it pushed her over the edge. She was off her head for a while.'

'Twins?'

'Didn't I tell you? Twin girls. Not identical, thank God, but I was the inferior copy. Benedicta was a beauty, like Mother. I missed out all along the line.'

'Benedicta?'

'Father wanted a boy, better still, two. We were a bitter

disappointment. When he saw what he'd got he fetched in a whole fleet of what you'd call carers these days and left us to them. Mother with nurses in one wing, us growing up, fighting like cats in the other, while he lived in the New York house and made more money. The thing was, Ben had Mother's looks but I had Father's brains. I made him send me to Vassar. He didn't like me much, but he was a fair-minded man, mostly. He saw my point, when I made it. I was doing well there, enjoying it, when I met Paul.' She handed her glass to Helen who refilled it.

'What happened?'

'Love at first sight. Crazy. Wonderful. I went up after the reading and told him how much I liked his poetry. He looked at me. I looked at him. That was it. Lord, it was mad. We were mad. It was 1938, the summer of my final year. I just cut and ran and went on the tour with him. Wonderful days. There really are times you know are the happiest days of your life. We knew. He was on his way west: Chicago, Minneapolis, the coast. Hotels booked all the way, of course. We just shared. The trains were more of a problem, but that's where my money came in.'

'What did your parents say?'

'Mother didn't give a damn. She was busy with Ben's engagement party. Ben had done the right thing, Ben always did. She had found herself a third generation financier from Boston and Mother was in trousseau heaven. All she said when I phoned her from Chicago was that I had better bring my poet to the engagement party. Father was a bit more difficult, but there wasn't much he could do really. He'd always thought going to Vassar was idiotic, so why should he care that I didn't finish? And he'd settled money on Ben and me years before, for tax reasons, so that was no problem. Oh, how we lived, Paul and I. I remember, in San Francisco . . .' The glass was tilting in her hand and Helen got up and took it gently from her as she drifted off to sleep.

She looked immensely old, skeleton bones showing through brown skin, but Helen also thought that she looked a little better, more relaxed. Had that furious outburst done her good? Here was another question for Dr Braddock, if he ever came back. Perhaps she should go and see him? If she stayed. She looked at her watch: seven o'clock. She picked up the glasses and went down to bless the microwave and make the kind of little supper of fish fillets and caper sauce that her mother had liked. Peas, also from the deep freeze, a spoon to make eating easier, and fresh bread and butter. She wished now that she had thought to look for fruit in Mr Patel's crowded little shop, but remembered that she had tucked an unopened packet of dates into the top of her case, refusing to leave them for the Dobsons to eat. She put the fish into a slow oven for its few minutes of blending and ran upstairs to wake Mrs Tresikker.

'You're real?' The old lady had been in a deep sleep. 'I thought you were a dream. I dreamt I was angry with someone, but I'm not, am I?'

'Of course you're not, Mrs Tresikker.'

'Oh, Beatrice, please. Easier now than later, don't you think? And you're . . . ?'

'Helen,' said Helen, and thought something had been tacitly settled. 'Your supper's ready, Beatrice. Loo first?'

'Yes, please.' There was a comfortable feeling between them of a rhythm establishing itself.

By the time she had got Beatrice settled for the night, the day had begun to seem endless. There were all kinds of things she ought to be doing, but the idea of bed was irresistible. She found it comfortable, meant to read a chapter of *Phineas Finn*, fell fast asleep.

She woke, late for her, to a grey morning and a cold house. She had left both their doors open, urging Beatrice to ring for her if she needed help in the night, looked in reproachfully on the way to the bathroom to say, 'You never called me.'

'I crawled.' Was it the first time Beatrice had smiled at her? 'You needed your sleep. And I feel much better. But it's cold.'

'I think the heating must be off.' Helen had noticed a blow-heater in the corner of the room and brought it out. 'You said you were having trouble with it?'

'Yes. Three Star card by the telephone, but I sometimes wonder if Wendy doesn't fool around with it. She does tend to know best.'

'I'll have a look when I get down. After breakfast, if you can bear it.'

'I'm not going anywhere. Did you sleep?'

'Yes. Do you realize it's Christmas Day on Saturday?'

'Does it matter?'

'No, I don't suppose it does. Except I'd better get some food into the house.'

'Mr Patel will be open all hours.'

'Yes, but you must have a butcher somewhere in Old Leyning. I prefer my food real.'

'Oh, so do I. Steven in the covered market. He's your man. Tell him I sent you. I always kept fillet steak in the deep freeze for Paul. And there's a vegetable stall across from him. Not Brussels sprouts.'

Downstairs, Helen found the heating controls at off, switched them on and was relieved to hear the roar of a boiler switching on. From below? A cellar? Investigating, she found the cellar door at the garden end of the hall, and went down to find the boiler rumbling away and, on the far wall, serried ranks of loaded wine racks. Now she understood the faint look of disappointment she had caught on Beatrice's face when she had taken up her tray the night before. She found a bottle of Burgundy, took it up to breathe, and set about making their breakfast.

No newspaper had come, and only one piece of mail, an obvious Christmas card. It reminded her that she had never checked through the pile of junk mail she had picked up the day before, and she collected it to work through with her second cup of coffee. Most of it was advertising of one kind or another, but she found two more Christmas cards and what looked like two bills, one from British Telecom, with a final look to it. The telephone had not rung once since she had arrived. She checked the phone in the hall and was relieved to hear the familiar ringing tone. But it made her realize that it was more than time that the two of them talked about money. She heated up the rest of the coffee and took the pot and the mail upstairs with her.

Beatrice accepted more coffee with enthusiasm and made a face at the mail. 'Christmas cards! Idiotic business. Thought they'd stopped coming. Throw them away. Difficult about the bills. Lost touch with the bank, rather. Used to do it by telephone. Mother's maiden name or something. Nice girls, kind, helpful. Then I got a letter full of numbers to use. And a – what do they call it? PIN code? It's around somewhere. I can't remember numbers, Helen. I meant to go into the bank, explain, but then I had the fall. Maybe if you could find the letter, take it in, they might tell you how much there is.' She was beginning to look sleepy again.

'Which bank?' asked Helen.

'Barclays in Leyning. That's the trouble. Up the hill, too far to walk, taxis can't park. Paul always banked at Barclays . . . My pension goes in there . . . Might be something in by now. Can't have you paying for everything. Must talk about it.' Her head fell back against the pillow.

Helen put the breakfast tray out on the hall table and began quietly searching the room, tidying as she went.

It was a bit like being an archaeologist, she thought, as she worked her way through layers of abandoned clothing, newspapers, books and mail. Beatrice Tresikker must have been very far from well for some time, just managing to keep chaos at bay with the weekly help of Wendy, who should come tomorrow. Then there had come the fall and the pace of confusion had accelerated. No mail had been opened for over two weeks, and Helen was glad to find a bank statement among this batch, as well as a couple more bills.

'Been busy, haven't you? Anything interesting?' Beatrice's eyes sparkled as she pulled herself up a little in the bed. Each time she woke from one of her short sleeps, she looked a little better.

'Yes, a bank statement. Unopened.' She held it out. 'And I found their letter, too, about telephone banking.'

'Splendid, then you had better go and sort them out. No, no.' She waved the envelopes away. 'I don't want them. You're in charge now. Open it up, Helen, and tell me how we stand. Red or black?'

'Black, but not very.' Helen was studying the brief statement. No money had come in at all in the month it covered, and only two cheques were recorded, each for fifty pounds, but several sums had gone out on standing orders – two, she noticed, to the British Red Cross, one for twenty and the other for fifty pounds. 'Your balance is only £250,' she said. 'And that was a while ago.'

'Not much riotous living in that,' said Beatrice. 'Better move something from deposit. My trust money goes straight in there.'

'Trust?'

'That was the joke on me. On Paul and me. Father left a mean will. I never for a moment imagined he'd do such a thing. He said I had acted irresponsibly. Not fit to handle money. Left most of it to Ben and her financier, set up a trust for me. Quarterly payments and the capital to go to my children, or if not, Ben's, when I died. What a laugh. Not much chance of it being children of mine!'

'Has your sister got children?'

'I don't know. How should I? I cut the connection, didn't I? Anyway, I shan't be here to care. But it made Paul terribly angry. He thought he and Pa had got on at that terrible engagement party. Well, Ben's Richard Norton was such a visible old Bostonian drip, it stood to reason Paul would shine by comparison. A long time ago.' She was beginning to drift again.

Helen had been studying the instructions for the new telephone banking system. 'I can see why you boggled at remembering all these numbers,' she said. 'If I got you a piece of writing paper do you think you could do me a note to your bank manager? I think we need an up to date statement of your accounts and a note of all these standing orders you seem to have authorized.'

'Not a bank manager any more,' said Beatrice sleepily. 'A personal banker, such nice girls. Yes, do go and see one of them. Explain . . .'

The doorbell rang, making them both start. 'I'm not at home,' Beatrice said as Helen left the room.

It was Dr Braddock, black bag in hand, into the house already. 'I thought I'd just come and make sure she was going along all right,' he said, starting up the stairs.

'I'm glad you did,' said Helen following him. 'And can we have a quick word afterwards?'

'If it is quick.' He was in the upstairs hall, knocking on the open door of Beatrice's room. 'It's Hugh Braddock, Mrs Tresikker.' He went in and shut the door gently but firmly behind him.

Helen fought down unreasonable fury. Of course he was in a hurry. Doctors always were. Naturally he had every right to see his patient alone. She stood in the hall, fuming, trying to sort out the questions she wanted to ask him.

'Much better,' he said, emerging from the room five minutes later. 'But you're no fool, you know that. Tell me, how long can you stay?'

Helen opened the door of the front parlour, glad she had dusted it. 'As long as she needs me,' she told him curtly. 'I lost my job. She advertised. It's a life-saver for me. Badly needed board and lodging. But I'm glad you brought it up, Dr Braddock, because I'm a little anxious about the way she is trusting me, taking me for granted. Someone needs to take up my references.'

'Well, she's not going to.'

'I can see that. I'm really glad you came. She seems to have nobody, nobody at all.'

'It happens. If you're worried, you had better go and see her solicitors, Finch & Finch in the High Street.'

'Old Leyning or New?'

'Old. They'll be in the book.'

'Yes. She really is better, isn't she?'

'Much. Whatever you've been doing, go on. Painkillers when she wants them. Let her do just as much or as little as she pleases. She has a lot of sense. Feed her up, let her rest, let me know if there is any change.' He moved to go.

'But the fall,' she protested. 'Has she been X-rayed? Is she going to be able to walk?'

'Oh, I think so; she says it's much easier today. I was afraid at first it might mean a hip replacement, and I very much doubt if she is up to that. Or to the hassle of an X-ray, come to that. All that waiting around. Anyway, she'd have refused to go, she made that clear enough from the start. I do try to listen to my patients, Miss Wesley.'

'Westley,' she said. 'Helen Westley.'

'Good,' he said, as if that settled something, and left.

'Maddening man.' She returned, still bristling, to Beatrice's room. 'Surely even a doctor should have time for basic good manners.'

'Why?' asked Beatrice. 'No one else has. It's not a mannerly world. Anyway, he did me good, and I'm the patient. He says what I need is a stick and some courage. I chipped the bone, he thinks, so it'll hurt, but it doesn't matter. Not a sinister sign of anything. Funny thing, at my time of life, you are always looking out for sinister signs, and yet what you really long for is death. Or do we? It's been a long morning, Helen. I don't know about you, but I fancy a glass of sherry before lunch.'

'Lunch?' Helen looked at her watch. 'Goodness gracious. And I meant to go out shopping.'

'I'm sure you'll manage another miracle meal for us. The shopping will just have to wait; I really need that sherry.'

Taking her first sip, she looked at Helen. 'He said a dreadful thing to me, that fool doctor. He told me I was good for years yet, if I was careful. I don't want years yet! Why should I? What am I to do with them? What have I ever done?'

'I don't know.' Helen gave up all thought of the shopping and poured herself a glass of sherry too. 'You tell me.' She pulled up a comfortable chair and sat down by the bed.

'Wasted my life, that's what I've done. Sat around waiting for Paul to come back when I should have been out in the world doing something. Being someone. Helping someone.'

'Why didn't you?'

'Every time I got started on something, he came back. Wanting me. Needing me.' She put down her glass with a click on the bedside table. 'Or needing my money? All this talk about bank accounts has made me think.' She looked cheerlessly at Helen. 'My father was right, you know. The last time Paul came back I had to tell him my capital was used up. Gone. Finished. We were down to the quarterly stipend. Not Paul's scene at all. He loved the large gesture, did Paul.'

What in the world to say? 'Was that long ago?'

'Ages. Let me see; time gets so muddly when you are my age. Ten years, fifteen . . . something like that. It was after I had started to get old. I remember that. He looked just the same, but I could see him thinking I had changed. Everything had changed. What with the money being tight and all, I suppose I had let myself go a bit. No fun dressing just for yourself. And after that time, not even a postcard. I thought it meant he had given up on the epic. I didn't realize for a long time that he had given up on me.'

'Do you think he is dead? You talk as if he were.'

'Yes, I had noticed that. Do you know that would be a relief, I think. I'd know where I stood: a proper widow . . .' She was falling asleep again, and Helen went quietly downstairs, seething with rage at Paul Tresikker, and made bowls of soup for them both. Too late today to do anything about the bank in Leyning. It was lucky she had drawn so much from the Mortlake cash machine on her way. She must find the shops and start laying in food for the long Christmas weekend which began to loom alarmingly near.

She found a stick in the downstairs cupboard and after lunch suggested that Beatrice try to use it to get to the loo while she was there to help. 'I never did like walking with a stick,' protested Beatrice, and the experiment would have been a disaster if Helen had not been there. It made her crosser than ever with Dr Braddock, but, 'Nothing wrong with crawling,' said Beatrice cheerfully. 'It's how we started after all, on all fours. You must read my book sometime when you aren't so busy.'

'Your book?'

'I've been writing it for years. About how the human race went wrong. Walking instead of crawling; men in charge instead of women. All a terrible mistake. Have a look at it some time. It's all in that cupboard, along with what I tried to write about Paul. A proper mess, I'm afraid. Longhand and pencil. Idiotic. Now, off you go and shop, and don't fret about me. I'll crawl if I must. That's the trouble about sherry, but it's worth it. Take the key with you, Helen. Hugh Braddock's been and I don't want anyone else.'

Before she went out, Helen telephoned Finch & Finch and was told by a brisk receptionist that Mrs Tresikker's affairs were handled by Mr Finch Junior, but he was tied up until after New Year's. Something about her tone suggested palatial offices, large bills and little interest in impecunious old ladies. Helen refused her grudging offer of an appointment in January and rang off. She and Beatrice would just sort things out between themselves, without expensive help from Mr Finch Junior. After all, she considered herself trustworthy. Why not let Beatrice trust her?

She found Steven the butcher lurking behind a mountain of turkeys. 'Old Ma Tresikker!' he exclaimed. 'I *am* glad to hear she's still with us. Yes, fillet steak, of course, and what about an order for Friday?'

'Isn't it too late?'

'Not for Mrs Tresikker. And I'm closed right through the weekend. I've a capon somebody cancelled. And she likes my sausages . . .' She found herself being talked through what seemed like a sensible, if extravagant, order. But, 'Feed her up,' Dr Braddock had said. They would worry about money in the new year. 'I don't suppose you deliver?' she asked hopefully.

' 'Fraid not. Used to. Hopeless these days with the traffic the way it is. No one does except Patel. Sorry, love.' He sounded as if he meant it.

By the time she had bought all the vegetables and fruit she could carry it was black dark. She had come by the lanes Mr Patel had told her about, a series of narrow passages and steps that led directly down from the High House, cutting across the zigzagging road. Now, heavily loaded, she stood on the pavement looking doubtfully at the first flight of steps. It was not just that it was steep, it was also very badly lit, just the place for a mugger. She sighed and started up the long slope of the road.

Four

S teak and a glass of burgundy were a success. By some shuffling of furniture and a good deal of running up and down stairs, Helen contrived to eat sociably in Beatrice's bedroom, and felt the shared food and wine a step forward in the acquaintance that was rapidly becoming friendship. 'Here's to Paul,' said Beatrice, raising her glass. 'And I hope he is either happy or dead.'

'How old would he be?' Helen had wondered about this.

'Older than me. Goodness, he'd be nearly ninety.'

'And nothing ever published?' Was it heartless to ask?

'Not that I know of. Not in book form. Lots of poems in magazines before the war: *Time and Tide*, *The Weekend Review*, *The Spectator*, that kind of thing.' She took a sip of wine. 'He used to write me sonnets, one a day at first. *A Garland for Beatrice*, he called it. Some of them made me cry for sheer joy. It was the most exciting thing that had ever happened to me.'

'But they weren't published?'

'At first he didn't want to. Said they were too personal, too private . . . And then there was the war, and it was all different after that. Looking back, I think Portugal was a mistake.'

'Portugal?'

'We went there, early in 1940. Paul had this rich friend

from Cambridge. A bit older, he'd met him through the Apostles, a port wine family from Oporto. A lot of their English staff left to join up, and he offered Paul a job at a Quinta – a farm of his upriver on the Douro. It seemed the obvious answer when the authorities were being so foul to him here, but looking back, I think it was a mistake. It cut him off, you see. No conversation; not with anyone who could stand up to him. And he hated the work. Luckily I managed to do most of it for him, on the quiet. I enjoyed it, learned a lot, even managed to learn Portuguese; I liked them so much. It was all wonderful for me. I loved the place, too. It was so beautiful, Helen: an old white farmhouse, set among vineyards, on the slope up from that amazing river. I'm afraid I was having such a fine time myself I didn't realize what was happening to Paul.'

'What was?'

'He was bored, I think. *The Soul's Journey* wasn't going well.'

'*The Soul's Journey?*'

'His long poem. It had a Greek name. Psycho-some-thing-or-other. Greek to me. I never could remember it. The trouble was, he needed someone to discuss his ideas with, cut his teeth on, and I was no use. Besides, I was so busy, so happy . . . Happiness is very selfish, Helen. I just didn't notice. Give me a little more wine.'

'Notice?'

'That he was drinking too much. We were surrounded by the stuff, you see. It was too easy. It began with port wine tastings, but it didn't end there. I think half the time when I imagined him wrestling with his blank verse he was dead to the world, sleeping off his lunchtime *vinho verde*. I only really noticed when the war ended and we got back to

England. And then it was all so wrong. His friends who had gone to the States had work to show for it; the ones who had stayed had been part of the war effort; we were out of it, sidelined, rejected. Worst of all, Virginia Woolf was dead. I hadn't realized that it was she who drew Paul into that circle, not Leonard. Myself, I had always liked him best; you could talk to him about anything. I felt she was always looking down her elegant aristocratic nose at me. So mostly I used to let Paul go off to Monk's House to see them on his own, it seemed easier. But when we got back, he didn't feel welcome any more. It was all change there and he wasn't part of it.'

'What happened about the sonnets?'

'My *Garland*? It was so sad, Helen. Nobody wanted it. Paul had been sure Leonard would take it for the Hogarth Press; that would have got him started, back into the swing of things. But Leonard didn't like it. Said it was old-fashioned; the sonnet was a dead duck. That was a bad day, when Paul came back from seeing him. He had walked all the way, over the downs, to cool off, he said, but he was still rigid with rage. He never told me exactly what Leonard had said, and I didn't dare ask. But he put my *Garland* on the desk in the turret room and never did another thing about it. And that was the end, too, so far as Leonard was concerned.'

'What did Paul do?'

'Plunged back into Psycho-whatsit. He'd been starving for books in Portugal and he rushed back to the London Library like a homing pigeon. I had bought him a life membership as a wedding present – they were amazingly cheap in those days. Do you know, I sometimes actually found myself regretting it when he began to stay overnight with friends because the books were too heavy to bring home. But I was quite busy myself. The house had been requisitioned by the Auxiliary Fire Service and they had left it in a proper mess. Paul's complaining about that didn't do him any good locally, I can tell you. So I was hard at it getting that fixed, as best I could with few workmen and less wood. And the rationing got worse. We'd been used to the fat of the land in Portugal and it did come as a shock. To both of us.'

'My mother used to say that the time just after the war was the worst of all.' Helen reached out and took the empty glass from Beatrice's shaking hand, glad to see that she had finished the pear she had peeled and cut up for her. 'What time does Wendy come in the morning?'

'Wendy? Goodness, is tomorrow Thursday already?' She was drifting towards sleep again, soothed by the wine. 'Nineish. She has to get young Clive to school first. You'll like Wendy.' Her eyes closed before Helen could suggest that it must be school holidays. Would the unknown Wendy bring her son? She set the alarm clock for well before eight, just in case.

In the morning, Beatrice was pleased with herself. 'I slept right through,' she boasted. 'All done by burgundy, and your cooking. I feel a new woman this morning.'

'You look better.' It was true. 'Does Wendy have a key?'

'No. I've kept meaning to ask her to get one cut, but she's so busy, poor girl, with all her jobs, and Clive.'

'I'd better get some cut today.' The list of things she needed to do before Christmas was becoming formidable. And the mail, when she opened it for Beatrice, made matters worse with a stark red final electricity demand. 'Whatever else I do, I shall have to get up to the bank today,' she told Beatrice. 'Pay this. Do you feel strong

enough to write some cheques, and a letter to the bank?'
They must talk about money, she thought.

'I'll have to, won't I?' The doorbell rang.

'You must be Wendy.' Helen hoped she was concealing
surprise as she gazed at the elegant figure on the doorstep.
Tall and slim in her grey trouser suit, Wendy looked like a
model off the catwalk – a black model. Her jet-black hair
was cropped close to her head, showing its elegant bone
structure, her dark face was challenging.

'Yes, I'm Wendy. The old lady didn't tell you? She does
like her little joke. How is she?' She was inside already,
taking off the grey jacket, rolling up scarlet shirt sleeves. 'I
was dead worried about her; meant to come in at the
weekend, but Clive wasn't well, my little boy. I'm glad
you're here. Answered my advertisement did you?' She was
in the kitchen now, opening the broom cupboard.

'In *The Lady*? Yes. Was it your idea?'

'Sure was. Beatrice jibbed at first – a total stranger, all of
that, but I put it to her that it looked like that or going into
care. Looks like we struck lucky. What's that?'

'Her bell. I thought it would be easier for her than
shouting. I expect she wants to see you. She's had her
breakfast.'

'So I can start up there, while you clear down here.' Her
quick eye had taken in the dishes stacked in the sink. 'I wish
I could give her more hours but she can't afford the money
and I can't spare the time. As it is I do the best I can in her
room, then down here, hall and stairs. Do you want your
room done?'

'No, it's fine thanks, and I'm not really organized yet. I
only got here on Tuesday and it seems to have been one
thing after another ever since. I want to get out while you're

47

here; she's a lot better but I don't much like the idea of her alone in the house for too long.'

'Still crawling to the loo, is she? You have to admit she's a game old bird. I hope you're staying.'

'I seem to be, but we haven't really sorted things yet. I thought I'd get her through Christmas anyway. It suits me, to tell you the truth.' She had stopped being surprised by Wendy whose upmarket speech matched her appearance. She had meant to go up with her, but now thought it would be more civil not to. 'I'd better get on with these dishes,' she said. 'I'll let you know when I go out. I have to get up to the bank and sort things there.'

'That idiotic business of the phone account,' agreed Wendy. 'What do they think we all are? Calculating machines? I thought of trying to sort it for her, but it probably wouldn't have worked. One must be realistic. Sex *and* race. You'll manage.' And on this note of approval she picked up the vacuum cleaner and went upstairs.

It was a brisk twenty-minute walk to the bank, first down into Old Leyning, then across the Ley and up the long sloping High Street to the top of Leyning proper. Helen almost wished she had summoned a taxi, but felt she was getting a useful feel of the little town, noting a bookshop, three chemists and more antique dealers than she cared to count. Once at the bank, she found a helpful young personal banker who looked little older than her niece Jan, inducing the first pang she had felt about the family she had abandoned. Liking the look of this Ann Simmons she decided the best thing was to tell her the whole story, as briefly as possible. 'The thing is,' she concluded, 'I want to share the expenses with her, but she's so vague about what they are and what she has.'

'Yes, I do see.' Ann Simmons had checked Beatrice's scrawled note with higher authority, male of course, and had it passed. 'I think the best thing I can do for you is to get you statements of both Mrs Tresikker's accounts for the last year. You're ordering them for her?'

'Of course. And thank you.' While they waited for the computer to run off the information and a list of standing orders, Helen told Miss Simmons about the problem of the phone account and found her sympathetic, but unable to help. 'It's a separate operation you see. It's all moving that way, towards automation. I really don't know how people like Mrs Tresikker are expected to manage, but nobody seems to think about them. My old Gran lives out in the country. They closed her village branch last year and I have to do all her banking for her now. It's a nuisance some-times, but of course I do it. I don't know what she'd do else. There, I think that's all you'll need. Let me know if I can help you again, but you'll have to come in, I'm afraid. You can't get through to us on the telephone since it's all been centralized. Some people don't like it much.'

'I'm not surprised,' Helen said, rising. 'I'm really grate-ful; lucky to have found you. I hope—'

'Yes, so do I. But I'm getting married next year.' It answered the unspoken question about how long she thought her job was safe.

Emerging into the High Street, Helen looked at her watch. Nearly eleven already. She had hoped to do a big Safeway shop on the way home, but the Christmas queues there were enormous and she must get a key cut for Wendy and catch her with it before she left. Safeway would have to wait until the afternoon, though the queues would doubt-less be still worse then. She was beginning to feel just slightly frantic with all the things that needed doing before the Christmas close-down and made herself slow her breathing as she had learned to do in an office crisis. How long ago that seemed.

She found Wendy dressed and ready to go. 'I have to pick up Clive from a friend's,' she explained. 'She goes to work afternoons and I mind hers. It's kind of split-second timing.'

'I do hope I haven't kept you?'

'No, no, dead on. Wonderful tidy you did in her room. Speeded me up no end. She wouldn't let me. But you've done her good already. Have a good Christmas.'

'And you. She paid you all right?'

'Oh yes. She never forgets that. And a present for Clive. She likes him. In the summer he plays in the garden and it's all much easier, but he'd go mad here, in this weather. Nothing for him to do.' Her voice changed when she spoke of Clive. 'I must run. See you next week.' And ran.

'So what did you think of Wendy?' Beatrice was sitting upright in bed, her eyes sparkling with mischief. 'Surprise you, did she?'

'She certainly did. I liked her so much, but it's awful she's just a cleaning lady. You feel she ought to be running her own show somewhere.'

'Clever of you,' said Beatrice. 'Her grandfather was an African chief, got himself killed in a revolution. Luckily for her father he was at the London School of Economics at the time, learning how to run a country, and marrying Wendy's mother, who was white.'

'Was?'

'They were both killed in a motor accident when Wendy was small. She's had a hard time since. And illegitimate Clive is hardly a help when it comes to discrimination. He's white as you or me, would you believe it. I think it's meant all kinds of trouble for the two of them. I've always thought they'd be better off up in London, maybe a more tolerant society, but the father's here, you see.'

'Who is he?'

'She won't say. Married, naturally, no children. He dotes on Clive. No wonder. He's a delightful little boy, well brought up, too. There's no nonsense about Wendy. How did you get on at the bank?'

'Better than I expected. I found such a nice helpful girl. I think she bent the rules a little for us. I hope I've got all the information we need.'

'Then pour us a glass of sherry and let's have a serious business conversation.'

Helen's heart sank. There was so much to be done before Christmas. But this was more important, and she knew she must seize the moment when Beatrice felt up to it.

'You'll have to do the thinking.' Beatrice took her first sip of sherry. 'If you show my mind a set of figures, it goes blank, and the darkness begins to creep in around the edges. I don't much like it, and it gets worse each time, or at least I think it does. It frightens me, Helen, not knowing whether it's worse or not, because of having no memory to speak of. I imagine you've noticed that.'

'Well, a little.'

'I'm glad you admit it. It makes things easier. Because if it goes altogether; if you see me turn into one of those poor old vegetables who nod their lives out dumped in front of a television set, or worse still, into hospital, blocking beds the young need . . . If that happens to me – and I think it will – I want you to put me out of my misery, Helen. Please?'

'But how?' Helen took a steadying draft of sherry and went straight to the point.

'That's the problem, isn't it? Hugh Braddock won't help.

Can't help, he says. Not that he doesn't sympathize. I think
he does, dear man, but he'd be defrocked, or whatever they
do to doctors who misbehave. And of course that murder-
ous Dr Shipman has made it all worse, brought out the do-
good interferers in force. I've given up even asking Hugh
Braddock so I'm afraid we just have to work it out for
ourselves. I rather think an overdose of paracetamol would
do it. Braddock warned me against overdoing that a while
ago so solemnly that I wondered if he wasn't trying to tell
me something.'

'But are you sure, Beatrice?' This was going too fast for
her.

'Very sure. If my mind goes; only then. I'm ashamed
now. I used to think, when I first got ill, that just being
unhappy and lonely and in pain was reason enough, but I
see now that it isn't. I worked it out sitting on the loo, when
I crawled there for the first time. I mean, why crawl – why
not just let oneself lie there and die? But one can't. If one's
still got a mind, I think one shouldn't. At least, I seem to be
still here.'

'Very much so. It's good to see you so much better. No
need to think about dying now; let's apply our minds to
how we are going to live.'

'Thank you for using the word. And promise, please. If
my mind has gone, you'll help.'

'If it really has. Yes, Beatrice, I promise.' Was she mad to
do so?

'Thank you. And now for our dreadful figures.'

When the friendly financial discussion was over and she
was making a quick, late lunch, Helen began to realize just
what she had done. After twenty-four hours acquaintance-
ship, she had tacitly committed herself to Beatrice Tresikker for the rest of her life. And worse still, to helping, if the

occasion should arise, in a suicide that might well be treated as murder. She ate her lunch very soberly.

'Regretting it, are you?' asked sharp Beatrice, when Helen went up for her tray.

'I don't quite know. I'm a little scared, that's for sure. And what I do know is that I must go out shopping right now, or we'll starve.'

'That would never do,' said Beatrice, composing herself for sleep.

Driving back from Safeway in a loaded taxi, Helen was surprised to see a car parked outside the High House. 'Looks like you've got a visitor,' said the driver.

'I can't think who.' She saw a dark figure approaching the house, caught for a moment by the taxi's headlights. 'Must hurry.' She paid the man quickly. 'I don't want her disturbing my friend.'

'Old Madam Tresikker? Don't fret about her, love; she's indestructible, I reckon. Thank you.' He took her tip and got out to help her up the steps with her load.

'That's kind,' she said, her eyes fixed on the woman who stood there. And then, 'Jan! What in the world?'

'Aunt Helen! Glory be. I was beginning to think I was on a wild goose chase.'

'A wild aunt chase? Not very flattering.' They were hugging each other, and Helen felt deep inner shaking in her niece. 'What's the matter, love?'

'I've left home. I couldn't stand it a moment longer. He was just awful when he heard you'd gone like that.'

'Your father?'

'Yes, and Mother not much better.'

'Oh dear, I did hope they wouldn't find out till after Christmas. I never thought they would. And by then I'd have decided whether I was going to stay or not, made up my mind about things a bit.' She turned the key in the lock. 'But come in, Jan, take your coat off, you look shattered.'

'I am a bit.' Jan picked up the Safeway bag the taxi driver had dumped on the doorstep. 'But all the better for finding you, Aunt Helen. Kitchen this way? What a wonderful house; how on earth did you find it?'

'*The Lady*. My mother always used it in a crisis. I suddenly thought of it, after that awful funeral.' She had followed Jan into the kitchen and they were both unloading groceries on to the big, scrubbed table.

'Wasn't it ghastly?' agreed Jan. 'Tell you the truth, I was worried about you. You looked pretty grim.'

'I felt it. The steak goes in the larder, over there. What a blessing he cut me such a big piece. You're the answer to prayer, Jan, actually. I was really beginning to wonder if I'd be able to cope. And the car too!'

'Won't they just be furious when they find I've taken the spare one,' said Jan with satisfaction. 'Luckily I'd been doing errands for Mum all morning and had the keys in my pocket. She'd gone to bed; Dad had stormed off to the office the way he always does, so I just packed a bag and left.' Upstairs, Beatrice's bell rang. 'What's that?'

'Beatrice Tresikker. I'm looking after her. A remarkable old lady. But how did you find me, Jan?'

'Oh, Dad had done that, raging and cursing and making that poor Miss Jepson give him your address. I really believe he thinks you've run away with a boyfriend, Aunt Helen.'

'What?'

'Funny, isn't it?'

'Not very,' said Helen. 'Call me Helen for goodness sake.' The bell rang again, much louder this time. 'I must run.'

'Don't run; walk. May I fetch in my suitcase?'

'Of course.'

Hurrying upstairs, Helen found Beatrice bolt upright in bed, scarlet with rage. 'You didn't come! What the hell's going on down there? Who are you talking to? I didn't reckon on followers!'

She was frightened as well as angry, Helen realized, and blamed herself bitterly while she bowed before the same storm of outrageous language that she had endured before. At last the note changed. 'And who the hell are *you*?' asked Beatrice.

'Helen's niece.' Jan stood in the doorway. 'Jan Dobson. And you're shocking my aunt. It's not good for you either, to get so angry, and I'm truly sorry I upset you by coming. Thing is, like, I'm an asylum seeker; run away from home, see, and if you'd met my father you'd know why. He's why Aunt Helen's here, really, and you need her, don't you? Please, mayn't I stay too? I'll earn my keep, I promise. You likely haven't noticed, why should you? But Aunt Helen's looking kind of flaky. She's been having a hard time with my dreadful Pa too. Perhaps she's told you. Oh, please don't start again—'

But as the old woman opened her mouth to speak, a tremor ran through her, and Helen and Jan, moving swiftly forward, were just in time to catch her as she keeled over and fell sideways from the bed. She was breathing stertorously and the scarlet patches on her cheeks were surrounded by an ominous white. 'How's your first aid?' asked Jan as they settled her back against the pillows.

'Non-existent. But at least she's breathing. Hang on to her, Jan, while I phone the doctor.' Luckily the number was by the phone, but would the surgery be open? It was not. She got a recorded message, which told her, miraculously, that Braddock was the doctor on call, and gave his number.

He answered it himself, almost at once, said, 'It sounds like a small stroke; do nothing. I'll be with you in ten minutes. Unlock the door.' And rang off.

'A man of few words,' said Jan.

'Yes. I like him.' Helen surprised herself.

Five

T ime dragged as they sat there, listening to the heavy breathing, but in fact it was less than ten minutes before they heard a car pull up, the front door slam, and swift steps on the stairs. Dr Braddock was in jeans and a heavy pullover and had obviously not even paused to comb his hair.

'I've been afraid of this.' He spoke to Helen as he checked his patient. 'Got herself worked up again did she? But she's very much alive. Only a small stroke. Won't she just be furious.'

'That she didn't die?' Helen understood him at once. 'I suppose she will. It was our fault she got upset; my niece arrived unexpectedly—'

'And she thought it was burglars? An occupational hazard of living alone. Don't waste time blaming yourself. You're going to be too busy for that.'

'But oughtn't I to be ringing for an ambulance?'

'What for?'

'To take her to hospital, surely?'

'Day before Christmas Eve? Where on earth do you come from, Miss Wesley? We empty our hospitals before bank holidays here in Sussex, not fill them. She'd only lie on a trolley for hours and most likely be discharged at the end of it. Anyway, I promised her years ago that I'd never send her to hospital if I could avoid it, and I mean to keep my word. But I'm glad you've got your niece here – there may be quite a bit of nursing for a while. Can you manage, the two of you, do you think, or should I try to find you some help?' He did not sound very hopeful of success.

Helen and Jan exchanged a look. 'Tell us what to do, and we'll do our best,' Helen told him. 'At least until the holiday is over.'

'Which holiday?'

'Both,' said Jan. 'Christmas and the millennium. If I may stay, Aunt Helen? I don't need to be back at college until the first week in January. But I don't know a thing about nursing.'

'You'll learn,' said Hugh Braddock, and gave them brief, firm instructions. 'It's a question of mixing rest and stimulation,' he summed up. 'You may not be trained nurses, but I'm sure you can grasp that. And, remember, if something should go wrong, and she dies, she would be the first to be grateful to you. But it won't. She's tough. Leave her alone; don't disturb her for anything. Bit of luck, she'll sleep this one off and wake up little the worse. If she does, tell her from me that there are to be no more scenes; she can't afford them. Mind you,' he paused in the act of closing his bag, 'she may not remember anything about it. In that case you will just have to play it by ear. But try not to upset her, Miss Wesley.'

'Westley,' said Helen. 'And this is my niece, Jan Dobson.'

'I'll see you out,' said Jan, but he was already halfway down the stairs.

'Wow, that was quick,' said Jan, returning. 'Does he never pause to speak? I wonder he has any patients at all, if that's the best he has to offer by way of bedside manner.'

'But he got here in less than ten minutes.'

'And made a lot of sense. So what do we do now?' They looked at the still, snoring figure on the bed.

'Leave her to sleep it off,' said Helen. 'Like he said. Thank God you're here, Jan. I wouldn't much like it on my own.'

'But if I wasn't here it wouldn't have happened,' said Jan as they started downstairs.

'Well, not just then, but maybe sometime worse. When Hugh Braddock wasn't on call. She blew up yesterday – all my fault. I went up to what was her husband's room – kind of a shrine, it is. It's a sad story, Jan. Lord, I'm glad you came.'

'So am I. Will you do something for me?'

'If I can.'

'Oh, you can all right. But you won't want to. Would you telephone Mother and tell her I'm here, and not going back. Well, only to pick up my things for college. I'll have to do that, but I'm not going to live there any more. Ever.'

'But, Jan—'

'You don't know what it's been like. Today's just been the last straw. Anyway, they never wanted me. Ask me, Mum did her best to get rid of me, never forgave me for hanging on in there. It was back to the social round for her the minute she could. And then nurses, then nannies, then boarding school for me when I was eight. Do you know what she did after I was born? Just as soon as she was well enough?'

'I remember she wasn't well for ages. No question of breastfeeding you.'

'No way. She was off getting sterilized so it could never happen to her again. I only found that out the other day, when they were having one of their rows, forgot I was there.

Trouble was, from what Dad said, it worked too well by a half; he never fancied her after that. Really, Helen, men . . .'

'Oh dear,' said Helen inadequately. 'No wonder they quarrel so.'

'And now of course they say they only stayed together for my sake. That's the last straw, after all the ways they used to get rid of me: boarding school, summer camp, you name it, I did it. So, from now on I'm taking that excuse away from them. Giving them the space to make up their minds about their own lives. I'm out of it.'

'But will you be able to manage? I mean fees? Living?'

'You've forgotten about Gran's will. Surely you remember the trouble about that? My A level year when I was revising like mad and trying to sort the conditional offers, and Mother didn't want me to go at all, and kept talking about a nice *cordon bleu* course, and Dad was having an affair with his secretary—'

'You knew?' Helen asked, horrified.

'Course I knew. And then, to crown it all, Gran's found dead in her bed in that great Yorkshire castle she lived in, and it turned out she'd left the whole rundown ramshackle lot to me. What a scene that was! It cost me my place at Oxford, but I'm not sure that wasn't a good thing. I'm in the real world now. I'd have left home then if I'd had any sense, but you remember what a boarding school baby I was. I remember going to the interview at Durham, in school uniform of all things, and looking at the others and thinking, "I'll never make it".'

'But you did.'

'Up to a point. Gran's doing. I remember when the first cheque came through I went straight out and bought the shortest black leather skirt in the market.'

'I remember it well,' Helen smiled at her niece, 'and the

row about it. But you never looked back. I always wondered . . .' She paused.

'Whether my behaviour was as outrageous as my clothes?
Clever of you. It wasn't. I'd seen enough of my father in
everybody's bed but his own. I'm waiting a bit. They call
me Miss Prism. I need a drink.'

'So do I. Wine do you? White in the fridge, red in the
larder. We ought to be making lists.'

'Tomorrow will be time enough for that. We'll have a
better idea of what we're in for.'

'I hope so.' She looked at her watch. 'Time to think
about supper. You must be whacked, and I'm all for an
early night.'

'In case she wakes. Yes, but honestly, Aunt Helen, I
couldn't face steak. If you'll call home for me, I'll make us
an omelette. Lots of eggs.' She had fetched the red wine
from the larder, found a corkscrew and poured for them
both. Taking her first sip she looked across the glass at
Helen. 'I thought I was gay for a bit.'

'And you're not?' Tread softly.

'I'm thinking it over. What I need right now is neutral
ground, and this feels like it, bless you and your old lady.'

'I'd better take a look at her. And then, yes, I will call
your parents, Jan, just to tell them you're here.'

'Thanks.' She reached out a hand to clasp Helen's. 'For
everything.'

Helen thought Beatrice's breathing had eased just a little,
and stood for a long moment looking down, wondering
what to hope for her. It had been interesting, and in a
curious way reassuring, to find that Dr Braddock knew
about her death wish. He might have refused to help her,
but he *had* promised to keep her out of hospital with its

threat of automatic, ferocious revival. Was it selfish to want Beatrice to live? She feared so, but could not help it. She wanted to know so much more about this interesting, impossible woman, and besides, she could not help thinking that Beatrice's death would leave herself and Jan in a proper mess. She had not even asked if Beatrice had made a will. She ought not to have let that wretched solicitor's girl fob her off. Too late now. She sighed, tucked the duvet more snugly round Beatrice's neck and went downstairs to telephone Jan's parents.

To her relief she got Marika, on whose consuming self-ishness one could always rely. 'She's with you? Well, that's a relief, though it all sounds quite idiotic to me. Frank's very angry with you, by the way, very angry indeed. Of all the thoughtless, inconsiderate . . . And what on earth are you doing down in Leyning anyway?'

'Looking after an old lady who's had a slight stroke. Jan is being the most enormous help to me, and has promised to stay until after the millennium. I really need her, Marika, and the car's worth its weight in gold.' She regretted the words the moment they were spoken.

'Outrageous,' said Marika. 'Taking it like that! How am I going to get to all my Christmas dates? That's what I want to know. Your precious brother has plans of his own, he tells me—'

'I don't think I want to talk about Frank,' said Helen. 'Surely you can hire a car for over Christmas—'

'But I've lost my licence.' Helen could hear her wishing the words unsaid. 'I was counting on Jan—'

'To drive you. I do see, Marika, and I'm sorry, but Jan has come to me, and we have a very sick woman on our hands. She will call you after Christmas to talk about coming to return the car and pick up her things.'

'What do you mean, pick up her things?'

'I told you. Jan's moving out. She's not said much about what happened there today, but it seems to have made up her mind for her. She's old enough to leave home; there's not a thing you can do except make the best of it, but I am truly sorry about the car.' She heard a door slam somewhere behind Marika. 'And if that is Frank, I don't want to talk to him. Jan will call you, after Christmas.' She put down the telephone gently but firmly as it squawked at her, and turned to see Jan in the kitchen doorway.

'Bless you and thank you,' said Jan. 'I'm just about to cook our omelette.'

By the time they had done the dishes and made up a bed in the small spare room behind Beatrice's, Jan looked worn out. 'Bed,' said Helen. 'Let's just have a look at her.' And then, closing the bedroom door again, 'I think she's breathing a bit better, don't you? If she rings in the night, I'll go, call you if I need you. You're bound to hear it, I'm afraid. Sleep well. I'm glad you're here, Jan.'

'So am I.'

It was still dark when Helen was wakened by the agitated ringing of the bell and then the sound of it falling to the floor. Pulling her dressing gown round her she hurried in to find Beatrice struggling to sit up in bed. 'Loo!' Her speech was blurred. 'Quick.' She was heavy against Helen, her left leg dragging, and it was an exhausting struggle to get her the few steps to her bathroom.

'I'm going to get help,' Helen told her as she settled gratefully on the loo. 'My niece is here.'

'Your . . . ?' but she was absorbed in her own relief, and Helen left her to it.

Helen found Jan hovering in the hall. 'Thank goodness,' she said. 'She's not very mobile.'

'Let's give the bed a shake.' They were silently relieved to find it dry.

'I meant to change it today,' Helen said as they shook the duvet and put it back.

'We may manage it yet.' A croak summoned them to the bathroom.

'I've brought my niece, Jan, to help,' Helen said from the door. 'She came last night. It's a mercy she did – you had a little stroke, Beatrice. Dr Braddock says you must take things very quietly and not upset yourself.'

'Pity I didn't die,' Beatrice managed to say as they helped her up.

'Not for us it isn't.' Helen saw her way. 'We need you badly, Beatrice. I'm homeless, as you know, and Jan is too. She's just run away from her horrible parents. She'll be off back to university in January, but right now she has nowhere to go.'

'Asylum seekers.' Beatrice's speech was slurring again as she settled gratefully back against the pillows. 'Send you back where you came from really . . . Tony Blair would. I shan't. Sleepy . . .' Her eyes closed.

'So that's settled,' said Helen out in the hall. 'What time is it, Jan?'

'Half past six. Might as well get up, don't you think? Lots to do.'

They were still writing lists over a second brew of coffee when the doorbell rang.

'I'll go.' Jan was on her feet. 'The post, do you think?' It was still before nine o'clock.

'How was your night?' Dr Braddock's voice. 'I thought

64

I'd drop in before surgery. See how she is.' He was moving towards the stairs as he spoke and Helen met him in the hall.

'Good of you,' she said. 'She's much better; slept through till early morning. A bit lame, a bit slurred—'

'But making sense?' He was ahead of her on the stairs now.

'Oh, yes. She said it was a pity she hadn't died. And that Jan can stay.'

'A useful conversation.' He was by the bed, reaching for Beatrice's hand to take her pulse. 'The breathing's much better.'

'We thought so. You're not going to wake her?'

'No way. Sleep's what she needs. Lucky there are two of you. She ought not to be alone in the house, but you'll manage.' He looked at his watch. 'Surgery starts at nine. Ring if you need me; I'm on call over the weekend. Call direct after hours, if you're worried.' He gave her the number. 'It's not listed; too many anxious old ladies. Not like her.' He glanced with what looked like affection at the figure on the bed. 'Best of luck, Miss Westley.' He was back on the stairs. 'I'll drop in anyway if I'm passing over the weekend, give her a proper going over when she's awake.'

'Thank you.' But he was out the front door, held open for him by Jan.

'Well!' she said.

'Surgery starts at nine,' explained Helen.

'If that's his office suit, someone needs to tidy him up.'

'He's on call over Christmas,' Helen told her. 'Which probably means he has no family.'

'No loving wife to press his suits? Yes, that would figure.'

The telephone rang for the first time when Jan was out shopping later that morning. When Helen picked it up and gave the number a woman's voice asked doubtfully, 'Mrs Tresikker?'

'I'm afraid she's not well. I'm here looking after her, Helen Westley. And you're . . . ?'

'Oh, that explains it.' Relieved. 'I'm your next-door neighbour, down the hill. We'd been wondering a bit, my sister and I. So much going and coming all of a sudden . . . Susan said call the police, but they're so busy these days, and Mrs Tresikker always did keep herself to herself. I tried to catch that hoity-toity coloured girl who cleans for her, but she said something about a hurry and brushed right by. No manners at all, but what do you expect?'

'My fault,' said Helen. 'I had made her late.'

'Oh. Oh, I see. We had begun to wonder if Mrs Tresikker wasn't being held prisoner in her own house. You never know, do you? Such a dangerous world, and all those refugees swamping the country. I was really relieved when I saw the doctor's car this morning – it was Dr Braddock, wasn't it? Dreadful, casual man, mind you. And what does he think is the matter with Mrs Tresikker?'

'A very small stroke. He thinks she is well on the way to getting over it, but we are keeping her as quiet as possible, Miss . . .'

'Oh, sorry. Fanshaw. Ellen and Susan.' The voice sounded more Roedean than ever. 'We've tried so hard to be good neighbours to poor old Mrs Tresikker, but she's a hard woman to help, as I am afraid you will find, Miss Westley. How are you managing in that shambles of a house? And what can we do to help? I always say that Christmas is a time for helping your neighbour. We'd be so pleased, Sue and I, to come and sit with her while you go out and do your shopping. You can't possibly be thinking of leaving her alone.'

'No, indeed. Dr Braddock said we mustn't. And it's wonderfully kind of you, Miss Fanshaw, when you must have so much of your own to do, but I have my niece here with me, so we are able to share the errands between us. You may have seen her drive past – a little scarlet Peugeot. She's out right now picking up the chicken from the butcher in the market. It's going to be a long weekend, isn't it, but we think we are pretty well sorted now, and Dr Braddock does say to keep Mrs Tresikker as quiet as possible. But may we call on you, if we suddenly need help or advice? It was so kind of you to ring.'

'I'm so glad you aren't kidnappers,' said Ellen Fanshaw. 'Susan really did fear the worst.'

Replacing the receiver, Helen heard the bell ring upstairs, and hurried up to find Beatrice sitting up in bed. 'Was that the telephone?' Her voice was clearer.

'Yes, your neighbour, Ellen Fanshaw, worried about you. Thought you had kidnappers in the house.'

'She would. Black ones, no doubt, all Wendy's dangerous cousins.'

'Quite right!' Helen smiled at her. 'Only she says "coloured".'

'Of course she does. Poisonous woman. Women. Tried to take me under their wing when they moved in. Ages ago. Coffee mornings and little chats over the garden wall. Lost my temper in the end . . . Thought that had fixed them for good. Pity . . .'

'You're much better,' said Helen. 'What would you like for breakfast?'

Jan was out all morning, and returned at last with a loaded car and a report of mayhem in town. 'You'd think they were shopping for the whole of the next millennium, and in

67

fact Safeway is going to be open quite a bit over the weekend, so we really shan't starve. Do you know the butcher actually asked how Mrs Tresikker was when he produced your order? You wouldn't get that in London, choose how. And how is she?'

'Toast and coffee for breakfast.'

'No!'

'Yes, and grumbled because I gave her the coffee in a mug, not a cup and saucer.' Helen was putting on her jacket. 'Is it raining? I'll come and help you unload the car.'

'Thanks. I got a few extra things . . .' On a note of apology. 'Seemed like we ought to have a bit of Christmas, and they had these tiny trees marked down at the green-grocer in the market. I couldn't resist it. Pot and all, you see.' She was extricating the little tree lovingly from the back seat of the car. 'For Mrs Tresikker's room, don't you think?'

'I wonder what in the world she'll say. And I thought you always said Christmas was an old-fashioned bore, Jan.'

'Well it was, wasn't it? I'm sorry, Aunt Helen, but you can't pretend those family lunches at your house were anything but a horrible farce, now can you? A bit of ritual tyranny, with you as the major victim.'

'Me?'

'Well, who did all the work? And got grumbled at for your pains if everything wasn't just exactly the way it had been for the last hundred years or so.'

'It was all right when Father was alive.'

'I don't remember him. I'm sorry. Which makes it a long time ago.' They were stowing the shopping as they talked. 'What happened to your life, Aunt Helen?'

'If you are going to ask me questions like that, I think you had better just call me Helen.'

'OK. You're easy to work with, did you know?'

'Well, so are you, come to that.'

'I suppose it works both ways. But you didn't answer my question.'

'Such a large one. And really you know the answer just as well as I do.'

'I suppose I do. Your mother ate it up. That's why I am leaving home.'

'Ruthless,' said Helen. 'But sensible, maybe. What shall we have for lunch?'

Six

'You'd better take an umbrella,' said Jan. The afternoon was already darkening by the time Helen was ready to go out and do her share of the shopping. 'Or the car, even. But the parking's hideous.'

'I bet it is. No, I'd rather walk, thanks. It's very quick if you go down by the lanes, and you get the most interesting views of people's back gardens.'

The umbrellas were up in Old Leyning High Street and Helen was glad to dive in to Boots for the supplies Dr Braddock had told her to lay in for the long holiday. She added a few necessities of her own and a bottle of *eau de Cologne* as a Christmas present for Beatrice. She must find something for Jan too, but wrongly chosen toiletries would not do. Waiting in the good-tempered, shuffling queue at the cash desk gave her time to think, and she went next to a little antique shop she had noticed, with a display of offbeat second-hand jewellery. Remembering well the family storm that had raged when Jan went off without permission and had her ears pierced, she bought a pair of flamboyant bunches of grapes made, the friendly assistant assured her, of semi-precious stones. Outside, rain streamed down now and the wind was rising. It caught her at the corner by the swollen, dark brown river and blew her umbrella inside out.

'Damnation!' She was struggling to push it back into shape against the threshing of the wind when a car stopped beside her.

'I'm going your way.' Dr Braddock leaned across to open the passenger door for her. 'It's no weather for argument. Whatever you've not done, leave it. You can't afford pneumonia. Crazy to be out in it.'

'It wasn't raining when I came out,' she said crossly, dumping the sluicing umbrella in the back of the car and settling herself beside him.

'Well it is now. You absolutely can't afford to get ill, Miss Westley. I'll run you back and take a look at Mrs Tresikker while I'm there. How is she?'

'Much better. Her voice is clearer and she's moving more easily. One of us can manage her on our own.'

'Good.' He swerved to avoid a pair of wobbling bicycles. 'Idiots! How long can your niece stay?'

'Until after New Year's. I've been wondering about that, whether I'll be able to manage by myself. Trouble is, Mrs Tresikker's not well off, and nor am I.'

'So it would mean my old enemy, care in the community.' He came to a sudden stop outside the High House. 'Cross that bridge when we come to it, don't you think?' He was out of the car already and she hurried to open the front door. Upstairs, she was pleased when he held the door for her to follow him into the bedroom.

Beatrice was dozing, but breathing easily now, and she woke when Braddock spoke to her. 'Better,' she said. 'Dammit.'

'Tough.' He went to work on her. 'You've got away lightly this time,' he said presently. 'More than you deserve. You must watch that temper of yours, Mrs Tresikker. You're none the worse that I can see – this time – but

71

blow it again like that and you may find yourself reduced to the kind of cabbage state you're afraid of.'

'Unfair,' she said.

'Who ever said anything was fair? And, talking of fairness, maybe you should think about Miss Westley a bit.' He closed his bag with a snap. 'Awkward for her, don't you think, if you were to die on her hands just after she had got here?'

'Oh,' said Beatrice.

'Just so. Take care of yourself; no more alarms and excursions. I'll drop in over the weekend.'

'How about a glass of sherry?'

'Nothing wrong with that. And wine, within reason.'

'No, you. Stay for a glass next time. Old-fashioned custom. I'm too sleepy now, but a Christmas toast? You're on your own as usual?'

'Naturally.' He was at the bedroom door by now. 'I'll see how it goes. If too many people overeat and panic I'll be busy. 'Bye, Mrs Tresikker.' He closed the door. 'I have stayed for a glass once or twice,' he told Helen on the stairs. 'When I thought she was really down. Lonely for her in this great house; pity she has no friends. I'm glad you're here.' Jan had appeared from the kitchen and he spoke to them both.

'Try to make time for that drink,' said Helen. 'She meant it.'

'And so do we,' said Jan.

'Thanks. I'll try to come.' He opened the front door and a blast of rain and wind blew into the house. 'Happy Christmas!' He slammed the door behind him.

In its strange way it was a happy one. Working together, Helen and Jan were getting to know one another and liking

what they found, and Beatrice Tresikker, to her own out-
rage, was getting better every day. The pain from her hip had
lessened and she was moving much more easily, threatening
soon to be able to get to the bathroom without help.

'Not yet.' Dr Braddock had dropped in on Boxing Day
morning and stayed for a glass of apple juice and a mince
pie. 'The last thing you need – for everyone's sake – is
another fall. Maybe by the time Miss Dobson goes?'

It was not quite a question, but Jan answered it just the
same. 'I'll have to go after New Year's,' she told him. 'I've
got a reading week fixed up, and a lot of organizing to do.
Will my aunt be able to manage on her own by then, do you
think?'

'I wouldn't be surprised.' He thought about it. 'If Mrs
Tresikker promises to be immensely sensible.'

'Not much option have I?' said Beatrice crossly. 'Do for
God's sake tell them to go out for walks together, Doctor,
and leave me alone. It's ridiculous, this nipping in and out
in shifts. The worst I can do is die, and that's what I want,
after all.'

'Have you made that will yet?'

The abrupt question surprised Helen for a minute, then
she realized that it was just to ask it that he had come.

'Well, no . . .' Helen had seen her furious, but never
embarrassed before.

'Then you can't afford to take chances until you have.
Think what a mess you would leave Miss Westley in, maybe
liable for your debts. Ah, got you there!' He saw that the
shot had gone home. 'Is it still Finch & Finch, or have you
quarrelled with them too?'

'How do you mean, "too"? Of course not. They're not
worth it.'

'I tried to get to see them before Christmas,' Helen told

73

him. 'But the girl said they were busy until well into the new year.'

'They won't be if you tell them it's a house visit for a will. And that I said the sooner the better. Tell them I'll meet their man here, act as a witness if they like.'

'Tell them I'm compos mentis still?' Beatrice pounced on it.

'Exactly. I've never beaten about the bush with you, Beatrice Tresikker, and I'm not starting now.' He finished his apple juice. 'Time I was on my way.'

'Thank you, Doctor,' she said, almost meekly.

Taking him downstairs, Helen thanked him too. 'She never told me she hadn't made a will. That's awful.'

'You'd be surprised how many people don't. Can't bring themselves to face the fact of death. Or take it for granted it will go to their next of kin anyway. And what a mess that leaves. Poor woman, you can see her problem. She must have told you about that vanished husband of hers. She truly doesn't know whether he's alive or dead. Awkward for her.'

'To put it mildly. Did you know him?'

'No, but I'd like to get my hands on him.'

'Something with boiling oil in it?'

'Exactly. If he's alive. I count on you to put the fear of God into Finch & Finch, Miss Westley.'

'I think your message should do it.'

'I hope so,' with one of his rare, wry smiles. 'I meant it to. Thanks.' He shrugged into his shabby raincoat and pushed open the door. 'Still raining!'

Back upstairs, Helen found Jan lecturing Beatrice Tresikker. 'My father made me make one when I turned eighteen. He even wanted to tell me what to put in it.'

74

'I bet he did,' said Helen. 'And I bet you didn't. I wonder if Finch & Finch will be open tomorrow.'

'Skeleton staff, I'd think,' said Beatrice. 'For crises. I hardly think this counts as one, but it has suddenly struck me it would be nice to leave something to Wendy. If there's anything *to* leave.'

'This house must be worth a packet,' said Jan. 'And some of the things in it, too. I've a friend who's into old furniture, and he says it's amazing what things fetch, if you set about it right. Have you ever watched *Antiques Roadshow*?'

'Television!' said Beatrice.

Her tone made them both laugh, but then they looked at each other. 'There isn't one,' said Jan. 'Do you know, I absolutely hadn't noticed.'

'Well, we've been quite busy.' Helen smiled at her. 'I did think about it for a minute yesterday. We always used to watch the Queen.'

'Did we not!' said Jan. 'One of the small tyrannies of Christmas. But just the same, I think while you are bashing the solicitors, Helen, I am going to be organizing a rental TV for New Year's. I'm not missing the millennium celebrations because you're still living in the dark ages, Mrs Tresikker.'

'If you don't mind . . .' Helen looked anxiously at Beatrice, afraid of another explosion, but the old lady was smiling.

'Not much use my minding, I can see. All right by me so long as you pay for it, and keep it downstairs out of my way,' she said. 'And now I want my lunch and after that I am going to have a sleep, and you two are going to go out for a walk together.'

'But Dr Braddock never said—' began Helen.

'He didn't exactly say yes, but he didn't say no either, if

75

you noticed, and this is something I am going to decide. It's my life, after all, and my death, even if I haven't made a will. I'll be thinking about it while you're out. My mind works better in an empty house. No offence meant, but it's what I'm used to.'

'I've been longing to do this.' Jan pushed back the bolt of the door in the high wall at the top of the shaggy garden. 'Amazing to have no idea of what's on the other side.'

'Well, trees,' said Helen.

'And a rookery. Yes. Wow, this door's stuck. Not been used for years, I suppose . . . Well I'm damned!' The door had swung open at last to reveal an overgrown graveyard.

'But where's the church?' said Helen. 'And do you think we can get across?'

'Of course we can.' They were both wearing jeans tucked into boots. 'There was a path once, look.' She led the way, holding back the odd bramble for her aunt. 'I wonder when they had the last burial here.'

'Not this century by the look of things.'

'It will be last century next week, how odd. Oh look, there's the church.' They had emerged from the screen of trees to see the little grey building hunched in a fold of the hill. 'It looks a million years old. I'd expected a cemetery chapel, all Victorian gothic.'

'Oh, no,' Helen told her. 'This is the site of an old abbey, well and truly destroyed under Henry VIII. My taxi driver told me. He said all the houses up here were built of abbey stone, but this looks as if it was an odd bit left over.' The path was clearer now as it approached the side of the little building and they were able to move more easily. 'Look, there's a new grave.'

'And it looks like the church is in use.' They had turned

the corner to see cared-for grass stretching down to the narrow lane that ended outside the church.

'Yes, twice a month.' Jan was reading the notices in the little porch. 'But not Christmas or New Year's.'

'Pity. I'd almost have liked to come. I suppose the door is locked.'

'Vandals everywhere. You do seem doomed to live near churches, don't you, Aunt Helen?'

'How odd, so I do. But better a church than a factory any day. I wonder if the path goes on.'

'Yes, look, with a footpath sign and all.' Jan had crossed the lane. She looked at her watch. 'Twenty minutes out and twenty minutes back, do you think?'

'Why not? Beatrice looked set to sleep for an hour at least.'

'You're calling her that?'

'She asked me to. "Better now than later", she said.'

'Sensible. But then she is. I like her so much. What a swine he must have been.'

'The husband? Yes, but poets, you know . . .'

'Poets?'

'Didn't I tell you? He was writing a great philosophical poem. He used to send her bits of it on postcards when he was off wandering the world in search of inspiration. I suspect they are all up there in the turret room waiting for the moment of triumph.'

'Or disaster.'

'More likely, I'm afraid. There was a sonnet sequence too, written for Beatrice, but Leonard Woolf thought nothing of it.'

'Virginia Woolf's husband?'

'That's the one. We're in Woolf country here, don't forget. That's why they bought the house, to be near them.

Oh, look!' The path had taken them through a little copse and now emerged on to a great sweeping view of open down, bare and grey and a little sinister in the winter light. 'She told me he used to walk over the downs to see the Woolfs,' Helen said. 'He must have started off this way.'

'A long time ago.'

'But nothing's changed.'

'Well, not up here anyway. What a wonderful place to live. Do you think we can get as far as the view from the top?'

'Let's have a go.'

But every time they got to what seemed to be the top of the hill it was to find yet another one rising ahead of them. In the end, Helen looked at her watch. 'I'm going back,' she said. 'I'm beginning to worry, and what's the use of that? You go on, Jan. Bring me back a report.'

'I think I will. Don't hurry, will you, Helen, it's too slippery.'

'No I won't.' She watched Jan for a moment as she turned and strode up the next slope, touched by her thoughtfulness. When had anyone last looked out for her? Self-pity. Disgusting. She turned and headed for what felt surprisingly like home.

'Glad to see you.' Beatrice had just wakened up. 'Loo, please.'

'That's a very nice child,' she said later as Helen helped her to settle back in the bed. 'You going to adopt her?'

'She seems to have adopted me,' Helen said. 'I hope you don't mind. And she's insisting on paying her own way in the most lavish fashion.' She had wanted a chance to say this.

'Good girl. Are her parents so very awful?'

'I've always thought so. Frank was much older than me, more like a bullying uncle than a half-brother. It was all right so long as Father was alive, he kept him in line, but afterwards . . .' She swallowed tears, remembering her father.

'Loved him, didn't you?' said Beatrice. 'Lucky.'

'Yes.'

'More than I did mine. And vice versa. Been thinking about my will. The one thing one mustn't leave is trouble. So I had a bright idea. We're going to ask Ellen and Susan Fanshaw to come in and act as witnesses. They are well and truly plugged in to the Leyning network. Convince them I'm sound in mind if not in body and there'll be no trouble. Of course, it will give them social ideas and you'll be fending them off for weeks, but I still think it will be worth it. Besides, you might enjoy them. No accounting for tastes.'

'I rather doubt it,' said Helen. 'But, yes, what a good idea. I wonder how early I should try Finch & Finch in the morning?'

'Ten o'clock sharp,' said Beatrice.

Calling sharp at ten the next morning, Helen got a woman's deep voice. 'Finch & Finch, Frances Murray, how can I help you?'

Not a receptionist. Helen plunged straight in. 'I'm calling for Mrs Tresikker, she wants to make a will, Dr Braddock says the sooner the better. She's quite old.'

'And I'm quite new,' said the voice. 'Could you hang on a mo while I find the file?'

'Yes, of course.' There followed a long pause while Helen heard the sound of filing cabinets being opened and banged shut.

'Sorry to keep you. I've got it at last. Mrs Beatrice Tresikker of the High House.'

'That's her.'

The sound of shuffling papers came down the wire. 'Yes, no will. There's a note about it, but no one seems to have done anything. Forget I said that. Look, I'm on my own here, holding the fort, but I could come in after we close, get a draft then, if that's all right.'

'That would be really kind. The thing is, she's not a bit well, had a tiny stroke the other day, and she doesn't seem to have anything in the way of family or friends.'

'It sounds as if she has got you.'

'I'm just the carer, really. I've only been here a few days, answered an advertisement. She was in a bad way when I got here, had had a fall, been on her own for almost a week. Actually I tried to get in touch with your office then, she's awfully vague about her finances—'

'And got the cold shoulder from our Eileen, I suppose. So she needs to know what she's got to leave before we can even start thinking about the will. There's a house?'

'Yes, big and run-down but a wonderful position.'

'Worth a bomb so long as it's free and clear. I don't see any sign of a mortgage or any of those old-age financial arrangements. I'll take a look at the file and make a note of anything that seems helpful. Then, if she cooperates, we can get a draft today. Have the whole thing signed and sealed right after New Year's.'

'Not till then?'

'This is Leyning, not London, my friend. Is she so very poorly?'

'Dr Braddock said, the sooner the better.'

'And he's no fool. There's the other phone. I'll see you

tonight, quarter past five or as near as I can make it. I've got the address.' And she rang off.

'So no need to summon the Fanshaws tonight.' Beatrice summed it up when Helen had finished reporting the conversation. 'But you liked her, didn't you?'

'Very much. No nonsense, and very helpful.'

'Like the girl in the bank,' said Beatrice, surprisingly. 'Perhaps you bring it out in people. Well, I suppose I'll just have to apply my mind to staying alive until after the millennium weekend.'

'Touch wood when you say that,' Helen told her.

Frances Murray arrived sharp at five fifteen and looked, in her neat legal black suit, younger than Helen had expected. 'You'd like to see her alone, I imagine.' Helen was leading the way upstairs. 'I'll be in my room across the hall, just shout if you need anything.' She opened the bedroom door. 'Here's Miss Murray, Beatrice.'

They had found a caftan that matched the duvet and Beatrice looked regal propped among gold and crimson cushions, in sharp contrast to the pitiful, desperate figure Helen had found the week before. 'It's good of you to come in your own time,' she greeted Frances Murray warmly. Helen saw her settled with a small table for her briefcase and left them to it.

Summoned by the bell some time later, Helen found them on excellent terms. 'Guess what, Helen.' Beatrice had a little colour in her cheeks. 'I'm not quite so dead poor as I thought. Father was a cagey old bird. Not very flattering, but then he never did think much of me. Do you know what he did?'

'No?'

'Left a second fund, not to be touched till I was seventy-five, or mentioned either. But there if I needed it. Funny old cuss.' She said it almost with affection. 'I wonder why he took so against poor Paul. Because that's what it all has to be about, isn't it, Miss Murray?'

'Not necessarily. No, I don't think you should take it like that. Rich men do get odd feelings of power over their money. They want to stay in control from beyond the grave, poor things. Not good for them, or for any of their connections. They tend to leave nothing but trouble.'

'My brother's like that,' said Helen, surprising herself. 'A control freak. But surely . . .' she had been thinking about it, 'shouldn't Mrs Tresikker have been told about the extra fund when she reached seventy-five?'

'Yes, I am afraid she should. There seems to have been some kind of an office crisis going on six years ago and the date just got overlooked. I've apologized to Mrs Tresikker on the firm's behalf, but I am sure she will get a formal letter from one of the partners. In the meanwhile I think it's the least I can do to see that she has her very simple will signed and sealed before the weekend.' She was repacking her briefcase. 'So if you could very kindly arrange for the doctor and the two witnesses Mrs Tresikker wants to be here at this time on Friday, we'll get it sorted.'

'Millennium Eve?' asked Helen, amazed. 'Are you sure?'

'Quite sure. I'm not a mad partier and anyway I've only been at Finch & Finch for a couple of months. Still feeling my way.'

'Like an Atlantic crossing in the good old days,' said Beatrice, surprisingly. 'Don't make friends too fast, you might regret it. Tell you what –' her eyes were sparkling – 'We'll be celebrating my new-found wealth. Why don't you plan to stay on and share whatever delights my beloved carers produce for me? I can guarantee it will be delicious. If you are agreeable?' On a note of apology to Helen.

'What a nice idea. Do stay.' She turned to Frances Murray. 'I thought a kind of small bits meal we could eat up here around the bed until Beatrice wants rid of us, and then we can go down and watch as much as we fancy on the television my niece, Jan, is providing. Do plan to join us if you really haven't anything else planned.'

'Not a thing.' Cheerfully. 'And I'd love to. It's good of you, Mrs Tresikker, but please, it's not wealth you know. Just a nice little nest egg.'

''Cause for celebration just the same. We're going to be paying bills like mad between now and then so I can start the new millennium free and clear. I can't tell you what a relief it is.'

'It makes me more ashamed than ever of my firm's carelessness,' said Frances Murray. 'I'll see to it you get that letter of apology, Mrs Tresikker.'

'From old Finch or young Finch, or even fledgling Finch? I never could decide which of them disapproved of me the most. I shall enjoy that. Goodbye Miss Murray, and many thanks for coming.'

'Mrs Murray actually. I should have said.'

'Then hadn't you better bring Mr Murray on Friday?' asked Beatrice.

'Oh, goodness, no, thank you very much. We parted a long time ago. But Finch & Finch seem to prefer married ladies.'

'Makes them feel safer,' said Beatrice. 'Murray your maiden name?'

'No. I'd changed my name at work once when I got married, drew the line at going through the whole hassle all over again when we divorced. Changing one's brand name is always a risky business.'

'Yes,' said Beatrice. 'Look at Consignia, poor things. Anyway, I shall call you Frances.'

Seven

'How on earth are we going to get rid of the Fanshaws after the will's signed?' asked Jan on Friday morning. 'Awkward, if we want Dr Braddock and Mrs Murray to stay.'

'Yes.' Helen finished her coffee. 'I hoped Ellen Fanshaw would say something about plans for the evening, but she very significantly didn't. Oh, well, there's plenty of food, and they may turn out better than they sound. Neighbours, after all.'

'There must be others.'

'It's the wrong time of year, isn't it? You don't see people much. Everyone just dives home to the television. I've been rather hoping that there would be a local Christmas card or two for Beatrice, but I suppose she froze everyone out years ago.'

'It might be a bit tiresome in a crisis,' said Jan thoughtfully. 'Having no one. Maybe we'd better cherish those Fanshaws. For when you're on your own. Where does Wendy live?'

'The other side of town. She cycles. Better in summer of course.'

'I liked her so much.'

'And wasn't Clive a surprise?' Wendy had brought Clive the day before, explaining that the friend who usually had him was ill.

'I'll say. Awkward for them both that they look so different.'

'Beatrice told me they had actually been stopped by the police. On suspicion of kidnapping.'

'Ouch. Even here?'

'Maybe more likely here. You don't see many black faces in Leyning, when you stop to think about it.'

'I suppose you're right. Nice old-fashioned, conservative little town.'

'Reasonably nice. Let's wait till we've met the Miss Fanshaws.'

'They're not the whole town,' said Jan.

'You look like a Roman empress.' Dr Braddock had arrived first. He smiled at Beatrice, enthroned in her purple caftan against golden cushions, and looked around the room. 'And what a transformation. You'd not know the place,' to Helen.

'It does look nice, doesn't it?' Ruthlessly tidied by Helen and Jan, and then cleaned by Wendy, Beatrice's room looked much bigger. Jan's little Christmas tree had pride of place on the big bookcase, and scarlet sprigs of holly drew the eye to Japanese prints on the walls. 'I do hope it's not going to be too much for her.' Helen was counting chairs with an anxious eye.

'I'll see it isn't. Don't worry. She's fine at the moment.' He closed his bag. 'Even the blood pressure. You're a credit to me, Mrs Tresikker.'

'And to my minders. There's the bell. If it's the Fanshaws, Helen, always early, don't bring them up till Frances Murray gets here. I can only take so much of those two.'

'Right.' Helen hurried down to find Jan helping two grey-haired women out of identical dark coats.

'Better early than late for an occasion like this.' The taller
one handed her scarf and gloves to Jan, as if to a menial,
and turned to Helen. 'You must be Miss Westley, the good
Samaritan. So pleased to meet you. And how is our dear
friend today? Does the doctor think her fit for this ordeal?
Though mind you, Dr Braddock – oh, thank you, my dear.'
Jan had whisked the coat off her back in what struck Helen
as a slightly ruthless gesture. 'Poor Sandra Braddock was a
dear friend of ours, you know, but perhaps the less said
about that the better.'

'The doctor is with Mrs Tresikker now.' Helen opened
the sitting room door. 'So we'll just wait down here until
Mrs Murray arrives.'

'Oh.' She had started to move towards the stairs at the
end of the hall. 'Of course. Deciding whether she is up to it.
Quite right too. This is my sister Susan. Miss Westley
and . . . ?'

'My niece, Jan Dobson.' Helen shepherded them into the
front sitting room, also tidied and cheerful with holly and
ivy and a scarlet poinsettia. 'Do sit down. Mrs Murray
from Finch & Finch wasn't quite sure when she would be
able to get away.'

'Not one of the Finches?' Disapproving.

'They are none of them working this week. I'm immensely grateful to Mrs Murray for putting herself out
for us like this.'

'Such a sad story,' said Susan Fanshaw. 'Oh, that must
be her.'

'Sorry to be late.' Frances Murray shook out her dripping umbrella and handed Helen a clanking plastic bag.
'Put them in the fridge for later? Is everyone here?'

'Yes, and Dr Braddock says she's fine.'

'Good. Then let's get on with it. I do try not to get

involved in things, but I'll be really glad when this will is safely signed, sealed and stowed away. Do me a kindness, would you, and winkle out Dr Braddock for me when we go up? I prefer to be on my own with the testator and the witnesses. Anyway the fewer people the better, for Mrs Tresikker, don't you think?'

'Of course.' She had hung up Frances Murray's coat and now opened the sitting room door to summon the Miss Fanshaws. 'We're not wanted, Jan,' she said. 'Mrs Murray thinks the fewer people the better, and of course she is right.'

'I should think so,' said Ellen Fanshaw. 'Such a very private business, a will, isn't it? Come along, Susan, we mustn't keep the old dear waiting.'

'No, that would never do. Suppose her mind should start slipping again.' Susan Fanshaw pulled herself awkwardly to her feet.

'There's never been a thing wrong with Mrs Tresikker's mind,' said Helen, more sharply than she had intended.

'Oh! Sorry, I'm sure, but I had heard some stories about fits of temper . . . ?' She was in the hall by now, face to face with Frances Murray. 'Well, Frances, it's been a long time. How are you, my dear?'

'Fine, thanks. And grateful to you for coming, but the less said about temper the better, don't you think, Miss Susan?'

'I had no idea Frances Murray was a local girl.' Dr Braddock had left to finish his round, promising to come back when he could, and Helen and Jan were in the kitchen putting smoked salmon on plates.

'No, what a surprise,' Jan agreed. 'It sounded as if she and the Fanshaws go back a bit, didn't it? More goes on in Leyning than meets the eye, that's for sure.'

'You can say that again. Goodness, can they be done

already?' There were sounds of movement upstairs, and she went out into the hall to see what was happening, feeling suddenly anxious for Beatrice.

Frances Murray was leading the way down the stairs, looking surprisingly handsome, dark eyes sparkling with what Helen recognized as rage. 'There you are. Good. Mrs Tresikker needs you. She's a bit upset.'

'Oh dear.'

It was awkward squeezing past the two Miss Fanshaws on the stairs, and they were not particularly helpful, with Miss Ellen busy trying to explain something to Frances Murray: 'Our duty as witnesses—'

'The doctor had taken care of that.' Frances spoke with strained civility. 'A witness's job, Miss Ellen, is to witness. Is this your coat?' But Helen had closed the bedroom door behind her and heard no more.

Beatrice was sitting bolt upright in bed, those alarming red spots flaming in her cheeks again. 'My own bloody fault.' She surprised Helen. 'Should have had more sense than to ask them. Pair of nosy old busybodies. Wanted to go through the terms of my will with me, didn't they? Make sure I hadn't made some kind of terrible mistake. Outrageous! Help me calm down, Helen? I don't want to foul up the evening for you all.'

Helen had taken the hand that clutched the purple quilt. 'Shut your eyes,' she said. 'Look at the darkness. Breathe slowly . . . That's better.' She slowed her own breathing in sympathy and counted its time gently into the hand that gradually slackened under hers.

Five minutes later, Beatrice was asleep. Helen settled her more comfortably against the pillows and tiptoed downstairs to find Jan and Frances sitting anxiously at the kitchen table.

'How is she?' Frances asked. 'Should we call Dr Braddock? It's my fault, I should have stopped them. Interfering old busybodies—'

'That's just what she said,' Helen told her. 'I think she's going to be all right, but it was certainly touch and go there. She's asleep now; I don't think we need call the doctor. He said he'd come back when he can, no need for panic stations. And at least you managed to get rid of them.'

'Shaking the dust off their feet, I'm afraid,' said Frances ruefully. 'I'm sorry about that. They and I go back a bit as I imagine you will have gathered. I did have a qualm when I heard they were to be witnesses, but as Mrs Tresikker had asked for them . . .'

'Absolutely.' Helen moved over to the fridge. 'Champagne time, don't you think? Jan, you're the expert.'

A cheering glass later, Helen ventured the question that had been teasing her. 'Do tell about the Miss Fanshaws. I hadn't even realized that Dr Braddock had a wife, let alone her being a friend of theirs.'

'Well, he hasn't now – partly thanks to them, I've always thought. A pair of troublemakers if ever there were such. Taught us all in the local school, and went in for favourites. Sandra Jones, later Braddock, was a natural born favourite. Film-star pretty, with not much in the way of brains but a gift for saying the right thing at the right moment. And an orphan, brought up by a bossy aunt, so we were all sorry for her, or tried to be, but it was difficult sometimes. Specially when she became such a teacher's pet. There was a bit of fuss about her A level results.' She looked from Helen to Jan. 'I'm being terribly indiscreet.'

'Safe with us.' Helen passed her the olives. 'All forgotten in the new year, we promise. And one must talk sometimes.

Tricky coming back to work where one grew up. Specially as a solicitor?'

'Yes. I'm beginning to think it was a mistake. But it's not so easy to get started. As a woman. So when Finch junior approached me, I jumped at it. Trouble is what they wanted was a token woman, and I'm not sure I'm going to be token enough for them.'

'Tea and sympathy,' said Jan.

'Exactly. Well, mainly tea. And running their errands. It's been wonderful, this week, being on my own. There'll be hell to pay, I expect, when they get back on Tuesday and find I've gone ahead with this. Not their form at all. They're great believers in gentlemanly delay. Makes them more respected, they think. I oughtn't to be telling you this.'

'Of course you shouldn't,' agreed Helen. 'But we're safe as oysters, quite apart from knowing no one here in Leyning, and you know it's doing you good. Oh, there's her bell.' She had been listening for this. 'I'll go.'

'Loo, please?' The red spots had faded from Beatrice's cheeks. 'Have you got rid of them?'

'Frances Murray did.' Helen helped her out of bed. 'She was furious. Well, so were they.'

'Pity,' said Beatrice as they shuffled to the bathroom. 'Not what I meant at all. Nosy old fools. Thanks.' She settled down with relief and Helen left her to it and went to tidy sheets and pillows on the big bed.

Settled back again, Beatrice smiled. 'Better now. Thanks. Glad that's all over. And now, did I hear someone mention champagne?'

'I'm afraid we've opened it already. Shall we bring it up?'

'Who's we?'

'Jan and Frances and me. Dr Braddock says he'll come

91

back later. We'd love to come and join you for a bit if you're sure you are up to it.'

'Of course I am now they're gone. I like that Frances Murray, don't you? She's a local girl, you know. Something about her I can't remember . . . Helen, my memory is getting much worse.' She reached out and caught Helen's hand. 'You won't forget what you promised me, will you?'

'I was mad to.'

'But you did, bless you. You've no idea how much better it has made me feel. Safer. Being sure I can count on you. And I can, can't I?'

'If the worst comes to the worst . . .'

'And I must be the judge of that. It's my life, remember.'

'But, Beatrice—'

'You promised, don't forget. It's my lifeline, that promise.' She smiled. 'Deathline. When my mind goes.'

'*If* it goes.'

'It's going. It's been my mind a long time, Helen. I know its little ways. Paul used to say they could use my memory for the national archives. I knew his poetry better than he did. All gone now . . . lost . . . vanished . . .'

'Do you exercise it?'

'What do you mean?'

'Your memory. Make it work?'

'What an odd idea. No, I suppose I don't. What is there for it to work on, stuck up here all day?'

'We'll have to think of something. I thought I'd order us a newspaper when things open up again. Maybe I'll examine you on the news every evening.'

'Bossy, aren't you?' said Beatrice. 'And now we have settled all that, where's that champagne? Please invite the ladies downstairs to join me in my salon.' Her smile lit up her face. 'Fancy you getting a promise out of sad Hugh

Braddock. I'd forgotten what a nice room this is. He says it's time I got up, by the way.'

'Good,' said Helen. 'I've been wondering about that. I'll fetch the others, but mind you tell us the minute you begin to feel tired.'

'I'll probably fall asleep,' said Beatrice cheerfully.

They had moved on from smoked salmon and champagne to chicken sandwiches and white wine by the time Dr Braddock arrived. 'You've got some catching up to do.' Helen thought he looked totally exhausted. 'Champagne or white wine? We saved some smoked salmon for you.'

'Later.' He had moved straight to the bed. 'You're fine, I can see,' he told Beatrice.

'More than you are. Sit down, for God's sake, before you fall down, and let them nourish you. When did you last eat?'

'Can't remember. At the hospital I think. Bit of a crisis there. Trolleys in all the corridors. The flu has started. The poor bloody health service is on the point of collapse again.'

'And so are you, Hugh,' said Frances Murray. 'When do you come off duty?'

He looked at his watch. 'Two hours ago. Champagne, thanks, but only one glass. I have to drive home presently.'

'Nonsense,' said Frances. 'I'll drive you.'

'Kind, but I'll need my car in case I'm called out.'

'Then I'll drive you in yours and walk back. It's no distance by the lanes and I'll enjoy it. Is your insurance still OK?'

'Oh yes, comprehensive as you can get. That's no problem.' He reached out for a second chicken sandwich. 'Do you know, I would be grateful, Frances. It's been a bad day.

No, I'll switch to white wine now, thanks. And not too much of that or I'll fall asleep where I sit.' He turned to Helen. 'I do apologize for being such poor company at your delicious meal. Just what I needed, God bless you. How did the signing go?'

'I near as dammit had another stroke.' Beatrice claimed his attention. 'And all you talk about is being tired and hungry. Those terrible women wanted to read my will. If Frances hadn't taken them away and Helen hadn't helped me relax, I might have died.'

He drained his glass. 'You're a thoroughly unreasonable woman, Beatrice Tresikker. You've been saying for months that you want to die, and now look at you.'

'Do,' she said cordially. 'I'm enjoying myself, aren't I? Never thought I would again. Helen's going to get us a newspaper and examine me on the contents every evening. And tomorrow I am going to get up and sit in a chair.'

'Good,' he said. 'But tonight I think it is time you had a little quiet, and I went home. If you really don't mind, Frances?'

'Of course I don't.'

'But you'll come back,' Helen said to her. 'And help us drink in the new year.'

'I'd love to. Are you sure you've had enough to eat, Hugh?'

'And to drink. Many thanks, Miss Westley, and sleep well, Mrs Tresikker. Where's Miss Dobson?'

They found Jan waiting downstairs with a plastic bag in her hand. 'Some spare sandwiches for you, Doctor, and a mince pie or two. Helen and I can't possibly finish them.'

'Ladies bountiful,' he said. 'I'd kiss all your hands if I was that kind of fellow, which I'm not.'

'Good God, pretty speeches from you, Hugh!' said

Frances. 'Come along home before you fall flat on your face.' The door closed behind them.

'They seem to know each other very well,' said Jan.

'Yes, don't they? It's odd, isn't it, coming in to a place like this, knowing nothing about anyone. Come and give me a hand tidying things upstairs, Jan? Dr Braddock thinks it's time we left Beatrice in peace.'

'She's had quite a day, hasn't she?'

'And stood up to it splendidly.' She absolutely must not tell Jan about that rash promise she had made Beatrice Tresikker.

Half an hour later, Beatrice was comfortably settled in bed, with Bach playing on the compact disc player Jan had given her for Christmas. She had been scolded for it, but scolded so gratefully that it was better than thanks. 'I shall fall asleep before it finishes,' she told them cheerfully. 'But the great advantage of it is it'll turn itself off when it does. Not like the radio at all. Now you two go off and enjoy yourselves and give my love and thanks to Frances Murray when she comes back from her errand of mercy. Clever of you to find me a solicitor who is an old friend of my doctor, Helen.'

'Yes, wasn't it? Sleep well, I hope, and don't let the New Year fireworks disturb you.'

'I like hearing the bells,' Beatrice said sleepily.

Frances got back soon after the other two had settled themselves with fruit and mince pies in front of the television to watch the millennium festivities sweep round the globe towards England. 'You missed the Queen,' Jan told her. 'She looked bored rigid, poor woman.'

'Well, the automatic pilot didn't work,' said Helen. 'We

all know how that feels. Did you get him safe home, Frances? Poor man, he did look tired.'

'Yes. And that house of his is an absolute tip,' said Frances. 'I couldn't bear it. Stayed for a bit to sort things for him. That housekeeper isn't worth the paper she's written on.'

'Does she live in?' Helen imagined some kind of confrontation.

'Goodness, no. Lives with a daughter who works, and a dozen or so grandchildren, and when one of them is ill she stays home and lets Hugh starve. Good thing you thought of those sandwiches, Jan, they'll help to see him through the weekend. That and the hospital canteen, but he says the food's terrible there. Oh, look, they are waltzing in Vienna!'

'Very stylish,' said Jan. 'How different from our own unfortunate Dome. But I mean to go and see it just the same.'

'Oh, so do I,' agreed Frances.

'Not me,' said Helen.

Eight

'I'm going to get up today,' Beatrice announced when Helen came to take away her breakfast tray next morning.

'You're sure you feel up to it? It was quite a day yesterday, what with one thing and another.'

'Those Fanshaws! Did me good, actually. It gets boring, just lying and thinking about oneself. But I don't think I'll try and dress today. There's a warm housecoat in the closet somewhere, or there was before you did all that tidying.'

'Ungrateful brute.' Helen went to the closet and produced a dark crimson robe. 'Three-quarter length, I'm glad to see.'

'Yes, I bought it with the stairs in mind. I'm reckoning to get to the loo by myself once I'm up. Easier from that chair.' Helen and Jan had manhandled a high, straight-backed armchair up the stairs for her.

The telephone rang and Helen reached out to answer it, rather expecting a Happy New Year from Frances Murray. But it was her brother's angry voice. 'That you, Helen? It's more than time I heard from that idiot daughter of mine. We've waited all week for an apology, her mother and I, and it's making Marika ill. So if you will just be so good as to fetch her to the phone we can get things sorted out, once and for all.'

97

'Happy New Year, Frank,' said Helen.

'I don't know what's supposed to be so happy about it, but the same to you, I suppose. How are you getting on with your mad old lady?'

'Beautifully. She is sitting in a chair right beside me as I talk to you. I am afraid you will have to wait a bit, Frank, while I go downstairs and tell Jan you want to speak to her.'

'Tell her I must. We're not standing any more of her nonsense, Marika and I, and so you had better warn her. I trust there is another phone somewhere in the house so I can have a word with my own daughter without your mad old lady listening to every word we say. Oh, and Helen, before you go, I've got a buyer for the house, contents and all. Fixed the whole thing up over Christmas without benefit of estate agent. Quite a saving, I can tell you. So I'd thank you to clear your stuff out of your room asap. Oh, and that reminds me, you weren't seriously meaning to go off with those two little bookcases, I trust?'

Helen took a deep breath. 'Indeed I am, Frank. Our mother gave them to me for Christmas and my birthday one year. You must remember that.'

'But she never meant you to take them out of the house! They are part of the furnishings of that room. And very nice little items too. My buyer particularly admired them, so I am afraid they are part of the deal now. Anyway, why in the world will you need bookcases now you are fixed up as some kind of carer in someone else's house?'

'Instead of being an unpaid one in our mother's?' She was almost too angry to speak. 'I'm sorry, Frank, those two bookcases were about the only really nice things Mother ever gave me and I don't mean to part with them. You will just have to find replacements for your buyer. And now I will go and find Jan for you, but do try and remember that she is over eighteen and her own mistress.' As she laid down the phone on the bedside table she caught Beatrice's amused eye.

'Your charming brother, I take it?'

'I'm afraid so. He wants to speak to Jan. Did you hear it all?' She had moved away from the receiver.

'He has a very carrying voice, your brother. Don't you think perhaps you and Jan should drive up today and rescue your things before he does something you'll regret?'

'But what about you?'

'I've been on my own before, remember. And it might not be a bad thing if you were there when Jan talked to her parents. Anyway, you'd better go and get her.' With an expressive glance at the silent phone.

'Father?' Jan exclaimed. 'Oh, hell.'

'Better get it over with, don't you think? Oh, and he wants me to take my things away. He's sold the house. Beatrice suggests we drive up together. Today.'

'Leave her alone?'

'I don't much like it either. But you'd better see what he says.' She started back upstairs as Jan reluctantly picked up the phone in the front hall.

Beatrice was looking pleased with herself. 'I got to the loo and back,' she boasted. 'No problem. I feel really better, Helen. Isn't it ridiculous? Not what I meant at all! So, no reason why you two shouldn't drive up to town today, face your gorgon and fetch away your things. I was thinking in the night that it was time we dealt with that turret room – or rather you did. I don't suppose I'll be climbing those stairs in the immediate future. So, if you'll clear it out for me, then, fair's fair, you store your stuff there. And Jan's of course, what she doesn't want to take to Durham with her. How big's her car?'

'Well, that's part of the problem,' said Helen. 'It's not her car, it's her father's, and he wants it back.'

'Better still. You can hire a van that's big enough to take the lot and make sure it comes with a willing driver who'll help with the carrying. Those turret stairs are no joke.'

'But, Beatrice, are you sure?'

'Making a will concentrates the mind wonderfully, I find. Of course I'm sure. Time all those clothes went to the Salvation Army, and then you and I are going to go to work on Paul's papers and see if we can't put something together out of them. With what I've done already as a preface perhaps? Better that way, I think. There began to seem something a bit grumbling about what I'd done of *A Final Account*. And anyway, it will be a project for us for the wet rest of the winter. What's the time, Helen?'

'Half past ten.' As she consulted the bedside clock she heard the downstairs receiver being put back.

'Then you'd better be off as soon as you can. Just leave me some more of those delicious sandwiches and I'll be fine.'

'But we might not be back till late.' It was only one of the many protests that were surging in Helen's mind.

'Then I'll be hungry. But not for a whole week like last time. You'd better leave me some bananas too. Just in case.' The telephone rang and Helen picked it up.

'Happy New Year,' said Frances. 'I hope this isn't too early for you. I do thank you for that happy evening.'

'Wasn't it nice?' said Helen warmly. 'And, actually, Frances, you are by way of being an answer to prayer. Jan and I need to nip up to London today to fetch away some stuff and we'd been wondering—'

'About Mrs Tresikker. May I come and spend the day with her? Would she let me? Could she bear it? May I bring the lunch and my knitting? And a book, of course, for when she gets tired of me.'

Some busy arrangements later, Helen and Jan were on their way to London, to meet the hired van at the house. They had decided on a self-drive one in the end, and lucky to get it, they were told, and very expensive it was going to be. But Jan had insisted on paying. 'My things as well as yours, Aunt Helen. You're saving my life, you know. I just hope we don't find Father at home.'

'I think I left him with the impression that we weren't able to get away until the afternoon.'

'Bully for you. But I'm still not looking forward to it. If Mother cries, I'm done for.'

'Oh, no, you're not. If the worst comes to the worst, you'll just have to go and sit in the van and let me handle it. Frances says they haven't a legal leg to stand on.'

'Isn't she a godsend. I loved the way she turned up, Scrabble and all, and took over.'

'Yes, a very capable woman.' Helen was glad the conversation had changed to this smoother channel.

'It must be a bit sad to come back to where you grew up and find so few old friends.'

'And a couple of old enemies instead. I wonder what really went on.'

Back at the High House the same subject was under discussion. Beatrice had greeted Frances Murray with enthusiasm and a demand for a glass of sherry.

'To drink in the new century. Not that it is really, in my view, till next year, but I'm sick of that old argument.'

Settled at last with her glass on a small convenient table with some of her favourite cashew nuts, she smiled at Frances. 'Now put me out of my misery,' she said, 'and tell me why those dreadful Fanshaw women hate you so?'

'Bad as that, do you think? Wasn't it awkward! I did wonder when I heard they were to be the witnesses, but there wasn't much I could do about it. And I have to say I had no idea it had gone so deep with them. None of it any of their business, and it was so long ago.'

'Yes, maybe. But remember you've been out in the world getting on with life, and they have been stuck here with not much to do, I suspect, and plenty of shared brooding time.'

'I suppose so. I certainly hadn't the slightest idea, or I think I really wouldn't have come back. Craven but true.'

'So what did you do to them that was so dreadful?'

Frances sipped sherry thoughtfully. 'They always disliked me. They taught us all at school you know, Hugh Braddock and Sandra Jones, who married him, and me. Sandra was prime favourite, always, and made the most of it. She knew just how to handle them, and you can imagine how the rest of us felt about that. I suppose we gave her a pretty hard time really, but I still feel she deserved every bit of it. And then we left and went our various ways. Sandra had these wonderful A level results we were all so puzzled about, but something went wrong at her Cambridge interview and she ended up at Keele, what a surprise. Hugh and I both got to London, which was what we wanted, and we saw quite a bit of each other. Concerts and theatres and driving home together for the vacation because he had a beaten-up old car and we could just about fit all our stuff in.' She paused and drank.

'Don't talk about it if you'd rather not.'

'I believe I'd like to. I never have. He was my first, you see. I was so sure it was for keeps, just taking it slowly . . . Happy, friendly times . . . We both saw other people, but we always circled back to each other . . . I thought I knew him through and through.'

'Such a mistake,' said Beatrice. 'What happened?'

'Christmas of our last year, Sandra came home from Keele with a broken relationship and a new hairdo and decided she wanted Hugh. You never saw anything like it. Straight for him, all sex-guns blazing. You won't believe it, but we hadn't slept together yet.'

'I see,' said Beatrice. 'So she got him?'

'Hook, line and sinker. He went mad, poor man. It was sad to watch. It was heartbreaking. It broke my heart. That's never going to happen to me again, Mrs Tresikker.'

'Life's full of surprises. Most of them unpleasant. So he married her?'

'Not at once. He had more sense than that, with all his medical training still to come, but it changed everything for him. He'd meant to fly high, go for a consultancy in one of the new, tricky, exciting genetic fields. He could have done it, too, such a waste.'

'He's a very good GP, and Lord knows we need them.'

'Everyone doesn't think so. That was his other mistake; coming back here. Her idea, I'm sure. She was always a small-town woman at heart.'

'What happened?'

'I've not the slightest idea. Oh, I hung around for a while, back then, I'm ashamed to remember it now. I just couldn't believe it would last. I'm still astonished, but it did. Until marriage. But I was out of the picture by then. I did have the wits to get out of London for my year's practical, got a place in a big Manchester firm, and they asked me to stay on at the end of it. Actually, I married one of the partners. And the less said about that, I think, the better.'

'Fair enough,' said Beatrice. 'It didn't last, I take it?'

'Last! It hardly even started. And you can imagine how awkward it made things for everyone. So in an awful way it was almost a relief when my father died and Mother got ill and begged me to come home. Her family have been blue-chip clients of Finch & Finch ever since the firm was founded. I think she probably put pressure on Finch senior. He's a lazy old codger, always was one for the easy option, and Mother was quite a bully in her way.'

'Was?'

'Oh yes, the joke was on me. By the time I had cut loose in Manchester and got down here, Mother was dying. Not such a *malade imaginaire* after all. So here I am, dogsbody to the Finches, stuck in a vast house at the top of the High Street, and the Fanshaws telling everyone I came back because Sandra had left Hugh. Which was not in the least the case, before you ask it! Mother didn't choose to mention that little fact when she was urging me to come home. She was a terrible matchmaker, was my mamma, but she knew me well enough to keep her plan to herself. I'd never have come if I'd known, and she knew it. Which does not mean that I am still pining for poor Hugh, which I am sure you are dying to ask.'

But Beatrice was asleep.

She was asleep again when Frances heard a car draw up outside the house just before five o'clock, and hurried down to open the front door and find Jan on the doorstep looking enormously pleased with herself. 'Victory,' she announced, glowing with remembered triumph. 'Helen just walked over them and, see, I've got the car. Dad said I'd need it for Durham. Helen's driving the van, but I lost her back at the turn off from the main road; she'll be here any minute.' She paused for breath and looked at Frances for the first time. 'How did your day go?'

'I'm a bit worried, to tell you the truth. We had a nice morning, talking, and then I read to her for a bit, and then she fell asleep so I went and made lunch, and when I brought it up she didn't seem to know who I was, or remember anything . . .'

'Ouch,' said Jan. 'So what did you do?'

'Jollied her along a bit, persuaded her to eat a little lunch, but halfway through she fell asleep and she's been dead to the world ever since.'

'Well, Dr Braddock did say sleep was what she needed.' And then, 'Oh, good, here comes Helen, and there's just room for her to park. She'd better hear about Beatrice before we start unloading, don't you think?'

'Yes indeed.' Frances was already moving towards the heavily laden van as Helen got out of it.

'Returning in triumph,' she said cheerfully. And then, 'But what's the matter? Is it Beatrice?'

'She's OK.' Frances hastened to reassure her. 'Been asleep most of the day. Still was when I came down. But it's her memory, Helen.' She explained again.

'It is going,' Helen agreed. 'I've noticed it, and so has she. I think it worries her more than anything. Oh dear, and you mean she may have forgotten all about having suggested we clear the turret room?'

'I think it's very likely,' said Frances gloomily. 'Oh, there's her bell.'

'I'll go,' said Helen.

'And we'll start getting things in while you explain.'

'Can you really stay?' asked Jan as Helen dropped her jacket in the hall and hurried upstairs.

'Of course I can. Where do we start?'

'The stuff to come in is all in the van. I didn't bring much in the end. By the time Helen had finished with the parents they were reduced to jelly, poor dears, and I didn't have the heart to do too much of a sweep out. I think actually Father must have consulted a legal friend between talking to Helen and our turning up, so he'd been a bit softened up in advance. Like he knew he hadn't a leg to stand on. It seems so odd they want me now after all those years of bundling me off to boarding school and camp and things, but I suppose I'm more use, now I'm grown up. And it turns out poor Mother has lost her driving licence for two years, so the car really isn't all that much use to her. Not without me to drive it.'

'I'm frightened.' Beatrice was hunched among her pillows reminding Helen of the desperate figure she had found the day she arrived. 'Helen – you are Helen, aren't you? I woke up and there was a complete stranger talking about sandwiches for lunch. Only she said she was my lawyer. Did I really make a will?'

'Yes, you did, yesterday, and there was a bit of a fuss about it and I'm afraid it has made you worse, a little. But you know me, don't you?'

'Of course, you're Helen, my guardian angel. And you've got a . . .' she hesitated, looking pitifully anxious.

'A niece, Jan. She and I have been up in London fetching our things. Do you remember you said we could clear out the turret room and store our stuff there?' She waited anxiously for the answer.

Beatrice thought about it. 'Did I really? Oh, poor Paul, he's really dead then? It came to me in the night that he was. I dream about him so much, but this time it was different. And we are going to write something about him, you and I. So I have to live for a bit. But, Helen, there is something else I do remember. You promised me, didn't you? If I turn into a poor old thing, with no memory and no control and no hope, you're going to dispatch me, aren't you, a parcel to infinity? You promised, Helen, I remember that.'

'And so do I.' How bitterly she regretted it. 'But we have to sort those papers first, remember, and write something about your husband. I'll enjoy helping you with that. Are you all right for a bit while the three of us get going? I'd like to get the van unpacked before it starts raining again, and Frances has kindly promised to help.'

'Frances?'

'Frances Murray, your lawyer. You remember. She turned out to be an old friend of Dr Braddock.'

'Hugh Braddock,' said Beatrice thoughtfully. 'Of course. How stupid of me. He was here, and those Fanshaws, and I lost my temper. Oh dear, I feel quite tired just remembering it. I think I'll have a little sleep while you get on with your unpacking, or whatever it is you want to do. I'm so glad you're back, Helen.' And she burrowed down among the pillows.

They worked like Trojans. 'No,' said Frances, 'like Amazons, better organized than the Trojans.' Bin liners full of once glamorous, now moth-eaten, men's clothes came downstairs and replaced Helen's possessions in the van to be dumped with the Salvation Army next day.

'What a blessing she is fast asleep,' said Helen, carefully sorting papers from the big desk into a vacated cardboard box. 'It will be a fait accompli in the morning.'

'I rather hate to leave you alone with her to face it.' Jan

turned from the closet where she was hanging clothes. 'But I did promise to get back for this reading week.'

'And of course you must. And honestly, Jan, I think what Beatrice needs now is a bit of regular quiet living.'

'No more millennia for a while,' said Jan cheerfully. 'I think it's what we all need. I have to say I'll be quite glad to get back to *Piers Plowman*. Don't you agree, Frances?'

Frances made a face. 'I can't say I'm exactly looking forward to telling the Finches about the busy week I've had. They're not going to like my having admitted to their mistake over Beatrice's trust.'

'Oh dear, will it mean trouble for you?' asked Helen anxiously.

'You can bet your boots it will be all my fault, one way or another. But honestly I wouldn't really mind a good reason for leaving them; it's never going to work out there, and we all know it. They simply cannot get their minds around treating a woman as a professional equal.'

'How long have you been there?' Helen asked.

Frances smiled at her. 'You've put your finger on it. Only two months. I can't afford to leave them as soon as that. It would look too awful on the CV!'

'I'm afraid you're right. Do let me know if there is anything we can do at this end to make things easier. Mind you, I'm quite sure Beatrice has forgotten all about the financial side of things. Will the new trust start functioning soon, Frances? She's pretty well broke.'

'I'll see that it does. And of course there will be a whopping great back payment to cover the time the fund should have been paying out. You'll be able to afford help if you need it, Helen, but don't forget you can always count on me. I feel I owe it you, quite aside from having taken such a fancy to the old tartar. I do hope she wakes feeling better in the morning. You don't have to go till Monday, do you, Jan?'

'I rather hate to go then,' said Jan, 'but I must. My reading week starts Tuesday and I've a lot to do. It's going to be a blessing to have the car, though I don't like taking it away from you, Helen.'

'Don't be ridiculous,' said Helen.

And, 'There's always mine,' said Frances.

Nine

The house seemed very quiet after Jan left. Dr Braddock, returning Helen's call with admirable promptness, confirmed her instinct to let nature take its course.

'She's been having a pretty exciting time, one way and another,' he reminded her. 'Just let her sleep it off, and try not to worry, but if you find you are, for goodness sake let me know and I'll come round and take a look at her.'

She rang off, thinking gratefully how different this was from her experience of the London Health Service, and looked about her for something to do while Beatrice slept. Resisting the temptation to spring-clean the house, she turned instead to the boxes of papers she and Jan had dumped in the front parlour. One contained everything from the turret room, and this she knew she must not even look at until Beatrice had recovered enough to give permission. Another held the files and papers of Beatrice's work on her *Final Account* of her husband's life, and this too she felt had better wait. But mixed up among these papers were folders relating to another project Beatrice had told her about, her book on women. 'You must read it sometime,' Beatrice had said.

This was the obvious place to start. Helen picked up a file labelled *Woman in Charge* and began to read. It proved a daunting task. Beatrice had written her notes sometimes in biro, sometimes in pencil, on lined yellow foolscap, and some of it had faded almost beyond recall. 'Homer was a woman,' ran one faint heading. 'Matriarchal societies', 'The White Goddess', and then, surprisingly, 'Shakespeare a woman: Anne Hathaway?'

The telephone rang and she was delighted to hear Frances' voice. 'How are you? Have you heard from Jan?'

'Yes, she rang the other night; safely back; sounded cheerful; everything under control. I miss her.'

'I'm sure you do. And Beatrice?'

'Still sleeping most of the time. I'm afraid we wore her out rather. How did you get on with the Finches?' It was after six and safe to assume that Frances was calling from home.

'Let off with a caution. You'll be getting an official letter about the second fund. And a whacking great back payment straight into the bank when they get around to it. They really had forgotten all about it, you know. There's not a sign of an automatic call-up system in that office. It frightens me. Back in the dark ages, they are, and not very anxious to move on. What are you doing with yourself, if Beatrice is sleeping all the time?'

'Missing Jan.'

'I'm sure. I liked her so much.'

'The house feels sad without her. But I'm busy trying to sort out Beatrice's papers. Lord, they are a mess, and handwritten too.'

'You need a computer; feed it all in and see what you've got.'

'You have to be joking. Until you can get those Finches to pay up we're poor as church mice, Beatrice and I.'

Frances laughed. 'I'll do my best, and in the meantime, I

tell you what. I've got a good, old-fashioned portable typewriter stashed away somewhere in the attic. It used to work well enough and I laid in a couple of ribbons when they began to be in short supply. Would you like me to dig it out and bring it over?'

'Oh, Frances, it would be a godsend. Don't you think Beatrice might react better to typescript than computer printout?'

'I'm sure she would. And you'll do a much better organizing job than any machine. I'll dig it out right now and plan to bring it round after work tomorrow, if that's all right with you.'

'Lovely,' said Helen. 'Stay to supper.'

'I'd like that, but let me bring something. There's a delicatessen up here that's open late. They do a fine line in quiches, just the thing for Beatrice, don't you think? Oh, and, Helen, something else I meant to say, though I shouldn't. Finch junior took a call from Ellen Fanshaw this morning. I was talking to the girl at the desk, she runs the switchboard too, and I heard her put it through.'

'Oh. I wonder what that means?'

'Nothing, perhaps. Whatever, I should hear something about it in the fullness of Finch time, and will let you know.'

'Thanks. Oh, there's Beatrice's bell. See you tomorrow, how nice.'

'Who was that?' Beatrice had been wakened by the telephone.

'Frances Murray. She's coming to supper tomorrow night. She says she can lend us a typewriter, in case you really want to do some work on your husband's papers.' Here was a chance to raise the subject.

'He's dead, isn't he? I remember that, though I don't remember how we came to know.'

'We don't really, Beatrice. It was just a feeling you had, but you have to face it, he'd be in his nineties, wouldn't he? Even for these days, when everyone has started living for ever, that's quite old.'

'Not as old as I feel, Helen. You are Helen, aren't you? There's a great swamp where my memory ought to be. Things come bobbing up out of it and then sink down again before I can catch them. Your niece – you have got a niece? I liked her, didn't I, but as for her name . . .'

'Jan.' But Helen's heart sank. Afraid of what would come next, she turned the conversation. 'I'm sure you remember the further past better, don't you? About Paul, your husband? We brought all his papers down from the attic, Jan and I, in case you wanted to do something with them. And there's another boxful from the cupboard over there. You said it was work you'd done for a book about him. You were going to call it *A Final Account*.'

'Did I tell you that? I must have been off my head. I was when I wrote it, I remember that. A black winter. I hated him for a while, Helen, after I realized that he had left me for good. Thought all kinds of dreadful things. Wrote some of them down. Funny thing. I remember, it did me good at the time; I felt better when the spring came, shoved it all in the cupboard and started work on my women. *Mother of Mankind*, I was going to call it . . . Nice title, don't you think, but as for that other stuff, Helen, please . . .' But she was nodding off to sleep.

Helen went downstairs very soberly and into the front room. She knew exactly what Beatrice had been beginning to say. She had been going to ask her to burn the papers from the cupboard. The black imaginings. And she was not going to do it. But neither was she going to look at or speak of them again, to anyone. Luckily the writing was so illegible that it was easy to make them into a neat parcel without reading anything. That done, she labelled them 'Beatrice on Paul', tucked them away in the cupboard that held Beatrice's collection of antique LPs and told herself to forget about them.

Beatrice slept all afternoon and woke looking brighter. 'We were talking about Paul, weren't we?' She took a sip of the sherry Helen had brought her.

'Yes. Jan and I brought all his papers down from the turret room, and we thought we might go through them and produce some kind of memorial volume. A small selection of his poetry, perhaps, with a preface by you?'

'It would do as a memorial for both of us.' Beatrice surprised Helen by taking the thought out of her own mind. 'Yes, I'd like that. The sonnets, of course, and some passages from *The Soul's Journey*, and a few of the occasional poems. Do you think we could do that?'

'I don't see why not.' Helen was delighted to see how Beatrice had brightened up at the idea. 'I tell you what; I'm going to get a notebook and biro and put them by your bed, and then when ideas bob up about your husband, you must write them down straight away, before they vanish again, like you say they do. And names, too, names of friends of his who might still be alive, so I could get in touch with them. What's the matter?'

'He didn't have many friends,' said Beatrice. 'Not after the Woolfs. After the war, he came and went so, you see. He used to get back exhausted. "To recharge his batteries", he said. He didn't want to see anyone; I had to cancel anything

114

I had arranged. I suppose that's how I gradually lost touch with people; they rather gave me up.'

'I see.' Helen's dislike of Paul Tresikker was growing so fast that she rather wondered if it would be safe for her to help Beatrice write about him.

And the sonnets, when she got them out, with permission, and read them, were not much help. Proclaiming devotion to the beloved object, they concentrated almost exclusively on the lover himself, his moods, his despairs, his hopes, his triumphs. And surely they must have been old-fashioned even when he wrote them in the thirties? The beloved was a nymph when she wasn't a nereid and her devoted swain a shepherd, given to rural archaisms. Helen could only hope that *The Soul's Journey* would prove more interesting, but so far she had found only scattered fragments, written in a tiny cramped hand on battered picture postcards from all over the world. Without some kind of basic structure, they added up to little but a few random and not very novel thoughts on life.

'What about your husband's early work?' she asked, two days later, taking Beatrice her afternoon cup of tea. 'The poetry that made his name at Cambridge? Some of that must have been published, surely? Jan and I only found manuscripts in the study desk.'

Beatrice looked puzzled, then wretched. 'I don't understand it,' she said. 'There used to be a drawer more or less full of little magazines he contributed to. How very odd. No one's been up there but Wendy and me, and anyway it's hardly the kind of thing that would get stolen.'

'Could he have taken them himself?' She hated to ask it, but thought it must be what Beatrice suspected.

'I think he must have. That last time he went was different, somehow. I don't think I quite realized how different at the time. If he had decided he wasn't coming back, he'd have taken it all, wouldn't he?'

'I'm afraid so. And I think he must have taken his outline for *The Soul's Journey* too. Well, he would, wouldn't he?'

'Of course he would. So it's no good, is it? We've not got enough to work on.'

'Oh, I don't know.' They needed this project. 'Think, Beatrice. Just suppose he's been holed up somewhere, writing away at *The Soul's Journey*, and it suddenly comes out, posthumously or otherwise, and makes a big splash. Then everyone will want to know about him. What we have to do is concentrate on your memories of him, get them down in some kind of order, and then see what we have got.'

'The life without the works.'

'Exactly.'

This worked well. Beatrice really did scrawl down notes of things she remembered, even dreams that seemed to her to cast light on her vanished husband and his work. As soon as Helen had got the house reasonably straight each morning she went upstairs, notebook and biro ready, to help Beatrice embroider on the previous day's jottings. Her memory for the far past was remarkable, a sad contrast to her grasp of the present, which was visibly slipping away. 'Jan?' she would ask, when Helen spoke of a telephone call, or, worse still, she would not ask it, but a hunted, haunted look would come into her face that warned Helen she was trying to remember and reluctant to admit that she could not.

She was surprisingly vague about Paul Tressiker's early years: 'He didn't much like to talk about them.' He had come from Liverpool, no money; she thought there was something odd about his father, his mother seemed to be in charge of the household. Then at Liverpool Collegiate he had been spotted by an English master, who took him under his wing, helped him with his Cambridge entrance. 'Got him in there, I think,' said Beatrice. It was with him that Paul had kept in touch, rather than with his parents, once he was safely at university. Oh, yes, they had been alive when she had come back to England with Paul but there had been no question of going to see them. 'He didn't even go to their funeral.' They were killed in the blitz, she explained. She thought it had been a relief to him.

She would much rather talk of happy moments on the trip west after she and Paul had first met. There had been a field of flowers in New Hampshire, a brilliant night at a lakeside hotel in Chicago. 'Oh, such happiness.'

But she always jibbed at talking about the visit they had made to the house on the Hudson river for Benedicta's engagement party. 'It was a disaster. I don't want to talk about it. I should have known better.'

'Did you like Benedicta?' Helen asked one wet Wednesday morning when they had been talking about what Beatrice called 'the disastrous visit'.

'Like her?' Beatrice thought about it. 'No, I don't think I did. I loved her, of course, my twin sister . . . but like? I don't think she was very likeable, you know. Maybe that's why I felt I needed to get away. She had to be the best, always, you see, have the best, did Ben. She didn't mind about Vassar, my doing well there, that wasn't her patch, but she wasn't best pleased when I turned up with Paul for that party . . . Her engagement party . . .'

As always happened, sooner or later, she was beginning to drift off into one of her catnaps, and Helen sighed with frustration, shut her notebook and went out to do the shopping. The belated cheque from Finch & Finch had finally cleared through Beatrice's bank account and she had invited Frances to supper to celebrate.

'Come into the kitchen for a mo.' Helen greeted Frances like the good friend she had become. 'I need your advice.'

'Yes?' Frances had expected this.

Helen poured their habitual drinks. 'Frances, I had no idea it was going to be such a lot of money. I don't quite know what I ought to do.'

'Like what?' Frances had settled on her usual stool.

'Don't you think we ought to get in touch with Beatrice's family in the States? Let them know she is still alive? Give them a chance to do something about her?'

'A chance to come over here and make her life a misery, do you mean? That's what she thinks would happen. Of course I raised it with her back at Christmas, when we drew up her will, but she was adamant she didn't want them to know anything about her. There's been no contact, you know, all these years. It must have been quite something, that engagement party of her sister's.'

'She didn't tell you what happened?'

'No. Just that they left the next day, she and Paul, and that was that.'

'But surely, Frances, the family could find her if they wanted to, through the lawyers and the trust. They must be in touch. She heard when her father died, after all.'

'Years ago. Anything could have happened since then. The trust fund arrangements are strictly between Finch & Finch and a Boston firm; nothing to do with the family.'

'It's wild, Frances.'

'Not really; just the way the law works. Specially in the hands of a firm like Finch & Finch.'

'Have they forgiven you yet?'

'Up to a point. They don't forget easy, those Finches. Mind you, I am beginning to think that Finch minimus might be quite human given half a chance. He's only a nephew, you know, not the direct line and rather there on sufferance. I've caught his eye once or twice when junior and senior were carrying on about the good old days when gents were gents and wondered if he didn't feel much the way I do. But he's very much on probation still, just like me.'

'Did you ever hear anything about that call from Ellen Fanshaw, back at Christmas?'

'Not a word. They are clients, of course. I checked on that, so it may have been something totally different.'

'But we both doubt it,' said Helen. 'There's Beatrice's bell, let's take up her glass of sherry, while the quiche heats up. It looks delicious.'

But Beatrice had wakened in one of her occasional bad tempers. 'What were you two plotting in the kitchen?' she asked querulously. 'Colluding and conniving down there! I never did like secrets.'

'Nor do I.' It made up Helen's mind for her. 'I'm sorry, Beatrice, I was asking Frances if she didn't think we ought to get in touch with your family in the States. It doesn't seem right not to let them know what's going on here.'

'You mean that I'm going off my head? And have them descend on me like a plague of vipers? Badger me into my grave with talk of wills and money and family duty? You don't know my family, Helen Westley. I do.'

'Well, you can't really,' Helen ventured. 'It's over sixty years, surely, since you left home? You may have a whole fleet of delightful young great-nieces and nephews by now.'

'Benedicta's brood? And that fish-faced banker of hers?

Two generations is much too short for any improvement in that stock. I was almost glad when Paul made it so clear he didn't want children. They might have turned out like my sister Ben. Poison. We won't speak of this again.' She drained her sherry glass. 'And I don't want any supper. Too tired. Go away, both of you interfering young bitches, and let me rest.'

'Oh dear.' Back in the kitchen, Helen looked ruefully at Frances. 'My mistake. What a fool—'

'No,' Frances interrupted her. 'I think it was worth a try. If the family comes down on us after her death as, frankly, they well may, we can honestly, both of us, say we did our best. And at least she didn't have another stroke, just got cross, that's something to be thankful for.'

'Yes. I was scared rigid.'

'So was I. When does Hugh Braddock come next?'

'Day after tomorrow, bit of luck. He often drops in after his Friday surgery and we give him a glass of something. He does her good.'

'He's a good man.'

'Yes. Damn, the quiche is burning.'

'Goodness, I'm glad to see you.' Helen had left a message with Hugh Braddock's receptionist, to make sure he came. 'I did a silly thing.' She described what had happened. 'I'm furious with myself. She's hardly eaten since, and slept a great deal, rather back to the way she was when I first came, except she ate then.'

'No work on the project?'

'No, dammit. She just says, "What's the use?" and goes to sleep again.'

'That's too bad. But, do remember, she's said all along that what she wants is to die. She may be beginning to. It

120

sounds a little like it. How much right have we to inter-
fere?'

'You say that?' She was amazed.

'Yes, I do. But only to you. Quote me, and I'm a done
doctor.'

'I shan't.'

'I know. I think I'll see her alone today, give her a chance
to grumble about you if she wants to. Maybe the sherry
bottle in twenty minutes?'

'Right.' She retired to the kitchen, surprised and angry to
find herself close to tears.

'And here's our sherry, just in time,' Hugh Braddock
greeted her arrival. 'I've promised Beatrice that there is
to be no more talk about getting in touch with the family, if
any, and she has promised me to have another go at living.'

'I'd like to see Jan again,' said Beatrice. 'I liked her,
didn't I? And spring. Maybe even a little touch of summer?
Are the snowdrops out yet?' She sipped at her sherry.

'Snowdrops?' Helen asked, baffled.

'In the graveyard out back. Paul used to come home
specially from town, when they were out. There's a passage
about them in *The Soul's Journey*, something about spring
and hope and revival. You haven't found that?'

'No,' Helen told her. 'But there are just a few snowdrops
in the back garden, so I bet they are out in the graveyard.
I'll go and look, if you'll promise to be good.'

'Not much choice, have I?' But they were friends again.

'Mind you go,' said Hugh Braddock as she let him out. 'I'd
forgotten what store she set by those snowdrops. That's the
worst thing about the poor bloody National Health these
days. No time to think properly about your patients, or if

there is you are just too tired. And you're one too, re-member.'

'One?'

'Of my patients of course.'

'But I never registered—'

'Don't!'

'No?' Surprised at his vehemence.

'All that red tape,' he explained. 'And no need while you are staying with Beatrice. But I've been meaning to read you a lecture on looking after yourself. You are Beatrice's lifeline after all.'

'That's what she said.'

'I'm delighted to hear that she recognizes it. So: Doctor's orders; you're to get out every day. Don't interrupt. Shopping doesn't count. A proper walk. Across the graveyard, or down the river, whatever. Fast as you can. Breathing. You're going to need all your strength presently. She's gone downhill a bit, this last week, no good pretending she hasn't. And I'm afraid I promised her all over again that we won't put her into hospital if we can possibly help it.'

'Ah,' said Helen. 'That's what cheered her up. I'm glad you did.'

Hanging their small wash in the garden on Monday, Helen paused to look at the little drift of snowdrops along the path. A gleam of sunshine picked them out and suggested that spring might really be on the way.

'I'm going to look for your snowdrops this afternoon,' she told Beatrice, settling her for her nap. 'Do you promise to be all right?'

'Give them my love,' said Beatrice.

The gate in the garden wall was harder to open than ever after all the rain, but this time Helen had brought secateurs and was able to cut her way down the overgrown path. Reaching the edge of the thicket, she stopped, entranced. Between her and the little church, all among the ancient gravestones, washed a greenish-white tide of snowdrops. Spring. A blackbird called a warning. Hope? She must bring her camera, try to capture this for Beatrice to share. Could she pick some for her, or would it be sacrilege?

She moved forward, very carefully, trying not to tread on a single one. Turning the corner of the church she almost ran into a tall, black man who was absorbed in cutting back the pervasive brambles from a grave.

'Sorry!' They both started back and exclaimed almost in unison.

Then, 'You must have come through the door in the wall,' he said. 'I've always wanted to see what's on the other side.'

'A garden.' She took in the clerical collar under his shabby windcheater. 'This is your church?'

'Surprising, isn't it?' His smile lit up the handsome, strong-boned face. 'It certainly surprised me. Nobody seemed to want this poor little church; talked of defrocking it; so sad to see one go. So I got volunteered. I've only just started but I'm having such a good time. Would you like to see?'

'Yes, please. But I'm not really a church-goer.'

'Not so much a church, more a group.' He turned to lead the way down the path beside the little building. 'I'm letting the sunshine in.' The main door stood open. 'It had stood empty much too long; so sad. Dry rot in the pews. We had to have a great clear out, as you can see, but it makes a wonderful space. Go carefully, there's a step down.' He took her arm to guide her into the dark, cool building.

'Not all that dark,' she said, surprised, as her eyes got

used to the light. Plain, greyish glass in the windows let in spring sunshine to show the simple, empty little building with its surprising dark red plastic chairs stacked along the walls.

'It's an undistinguished building, I'm afraid.' His tone was apologetic, he might have been introducing a plain, dearly loved child. 'Not a single feature for Pevsner. I think the locals simply cobbled it together out of the abbey ruins after the destruction. Even then it was handily away from the centre of things, you see. The heart of the town had moved up the other hill after the Black Death, to where the new church is.'

'New?'

He laughed. 'Yes, like New College. It's a good building. You've not seen it?'

'No, I've not been here long, and I've been quite busy.' She almost felt she was apologizing. 'I'm looking after the old lady who lives in the house beyond the wall. She's not a bit well. She told me about your snowdrops, she and her husband used to come every year. I was wondering . . .'

'You want to take her some. Of course. God and I can spare them. And when you say not well . . .'

She recognized it as a professional question. 'She's eighty, tired of life a bit, but doing fine till she had a fall before Christmas, a couple of little strokes, Dr Braddock thinks.'

'Hugh Braddock, that's good. I'm surprised he hasn't told me about her. May I call? She's in my parish, such as it is. I did have a go, when I first came, but I was ferociously turned away from one of those houses at the top of the hill, rather lost my nerve. I'm ashamed. I'm keeping you too long.' He had noticed her quick glance at her watch. 'Come and get your snowdrops,' leading the way back into the sunlight. 'You've left her alone?' And then, surprisingly, 'Quite right. It can develop into a kind of tyranny, the not leaving alone. The question is, who is being protected, and against what. You'll find the longest ones along the edge of the thicket.' He led the way. 'I confess to picking them myself for selected parishioners. Mind you, I look on the whole of both Leynings as my parish, really. This has always been a church for the protesters, the dropouts. I'm sure of that. Catholics creeping here under Henry the Eighth, Protestants under his daughter, Mary. Now I try to talk to doubters of all kinds, including, I sometimes think, myself. Try us some time. Ten thirty every other Sunday. And I guarantee to finish at half past eleven so those who wish can get the roast into the oven. There.' They had been sociably picking, side by side, now he handed her his little nosegay, reached into a pocket and produced an elastic band. 'When's a good time to call?'

'Mornings. Not too early. But she's no more religious than I am.'

'She's still my parishioner.' He produced a battered diary from another pocket. 'Wednesday, about eleven, and I'll plan to stay long enough for you to do a couple of errands?'

'Unless she refuses to see you. She can be ferocious.'

'Don't you think curiosity will get me in? There aren't that many black vicars in Sussex.'

'You're probably right.' She liked him better and better. 'She'll want to know all about you. Thanks.' She took the little bunch. 'They're lovely. I'll look forward to seeing you on Wednesday.'

'Here.' He reached into yet another pocket and produced a card. 'My number, in case she really does refuse. Don't fret about the unpronounceable name. Everyone just calls me Peter.'

125

Ten

Entranced with the snowdrops, Beatrice greeted the news of her proposed visitor with less enthusiasm, muttering something about bloody do-gooders, but Helen's description of Peter and his bare little church with its red plastic chairs caught her imagination, and she agreed to 'give him a trial', as she put it.

He arrived on Wednesday, prompt to his time, looking only marginally clerical in dark jeans and a roll-necked pullover. 'At least she didn't refuse point blank.' He smiled at Helen and handed her a tiny bunch of snowdrops.

'Not quite, but she's tired this morning, a bad night, I couldn't get her up for you, I'm afraid. And don't worry if she just drops off to sleep; she often does, in mid-sentence.'

'No problem. I always have a paperback in my pocket. It's a fine morning; don't hurry back from your shopping, I promise I won't wear her out. If all else fails I'll read aloud to her. Does she like that?'

'I'm ashamed to say that I don't know.' She opened the bedroom door. 'Here's your visitor, Beatrice; he wants to know if you like being read aloud to.'

'Very much,' said Beatrice. 'Poetry for choice.'

Returning from her quick trip to the public library, Helen saw at once that the visit had been a success. Beatrice was sitting very upright in bed, her eyes sparkling. 'Guess what,' she said. 'He knows about Paul. Found him in a footnote of Leonard Woolf's diary.'

'Not entirely complimentary, I'm afraid. Something about his gatecrashing a visit from Vanessa Bell. The name stuck of course; it's unusual. I'll look it up for you if you like, lend you the volume.'

'Yes, please,' said Helen. 'Did Beatrice tell you we are trying to put together something about her husband?'

'He says he'd like to help.' Beatrice took over. 'He seems to be a Woolf expert.'

'Not an expert, just a fan. I discovered the Bloomsbury group at university. I was at Sussex, you see, reading English among a lot of other things, you know how it is there. Naturally I ran into them, got hooked. You won't believe how strange, how exciting they seemed to someone with my background.' He looked at his watch. 'Forgive me, I must run. I've a date up the other hill.'

'Come again,' said Helen, seeing him out. 'You've done her good.'

'I'm glad. I'd like to. And I meant it about the research. I've reading rights at the university still. Anything you want looked up.'

'Wonderful.' She watched with approval as he straddled a battered old bicycle and rode off down the hill.

Upstairs, Beatrice was fast asleep.

'I liked him,' she said, waking for lunch. 'Clever of you to find him, Helen. I think we should show him the portrait, don't you?'

'Portrait?'

'Don't tell me I've never shown it to you!' As always when her memory failed, her face fell into a net of wrinkles that made her look a hundred years old. 'It's all I've got left of

Paul. He hated having his photograph taken; felt it stole a bit of him or something. Fetch it out, Helen, quick, it's time you met him.' And then, impatiently, 'It's in the closet, tucked away at the side. It used to hang where the Blue Mountains are.' She pointed at the Japanese print facing the bed. 'So I could see him first thing every morning when I woke up. And then one day I realized he wasn't coming back, couldn't stand it and took him down. Couldn't face him any more, too painful. Funny; I think I can now. I wonder why. Fetch him, quick, Helen. Right at the end on the left.'

The portrait was leaning against the wall of the closet, masked behind a black velvet evening dress that smelled of pot-pourri. Helen propped the large canvas against a chair and stood back to look at it. 'Lord, he was handsome,' she said. Obviously unfinished, done with broad, impatient strokes of the brush, it gave a vivid impression of a fair-haired young man who knew he was somebody. He was looking past the artist at something only he could see. Something that absorbed him. 'It's brilliant,' Helen said. 'Who did it, Beatrice?'

'Vanessa Bell. I always thought something happened between those two, way back. God knows what. She was old enough to be his mother. Anyway, she never finished it, never signed it, but it's him to the essence. Shall we hang it again while we're working on him?'

'Could you face it? All the time, across the room from you?'

'Good question. I'm not sure. Put him on the chest of drawers for the time being, and let's think about it. I rather believe I prefer my Blue Mountains to wake up to. There was always something disturbing about Paul.'

'I should just about think so. Dangerous for anyone to be so handsome. Was he charming with it?'

'Oh, the birds off the trees. Irresistible, he was. I used to enjoy watching it happen, at first, when I was so cocksure of him. And that's the right word, for sure. Oh, what a long time ago.' Her eyes were beginning to close, snapped open again. 'What colour did she make his eyes, Helen?'

'Blue,' said Helen, surprised. 'Why?'

'Then he was happy, sitting for her. Blue when he was happy, green when he got into one of his rages. I wish I could see better, Helen. People's faces tell you so much, and I can hardly make them out any more. That nice Peter, just a dark blur . . .'

'Have you glasses tucked away somewhere?' Helen had wondered about this.

'Years old. Totally useless. My optician retired and I couldn't be bothered to find another. It's all such hard work, being old, Helen.'

'We'll get you some glasses. Frances will know an optician. Or Hugh Braddock, come to that. So, what we have to do is get you walking well enough for the stairs, then Frances would drive you, I'm sure. Or Jan, at Easter. Hugh Braddock's been saying he thought it was time you were moving about a bit more.'

'He'll have me doing press-ups if I'm not careful. Bullies and tyrants, the lot of you.' But she said it quite cheerfully and might even have been smiling as she fell asleep.

Helen was with Beatrice when the front doorbell rang next morning. 'I'll get it,' Wendy called, turning off the Hoover in the downstairs hall.

Helen heard the front door open and then an outburst of furious, incomprehensible speech from Wendy.

'What on earth . . . ?' She hurried to the top of the stairs as a man's voice replied, equally incomprehensible, but sonorously calm. Peter. Of course. She hurried down to find him standing in the doorway, still trying to get Wendy to take the book he was holding out to her.

'Here's Miss Westley,' he interrupted as Wendy began another unintelligible tirade. 'We don't want to inflict our little local difficulties on her, do we? We're in England now, remember.' And, to Helen, 'Forgive us, please. We go rather a long way back.'

'You've met before?'

'No way. We don't need to have. Our tribal difference is built into our bones. But this is neutral ground,' to Wendy. 'Doubly so, both as England and Mrs Tresikker's house.' The bell, ringing upstairs, confirmed this.

'You'd better go up and explain to her,' said Helen, seeing this as the best way of separating them. 'Come into the kitchen a minute, Wendy?'

'I'm sorry.' Wendy spoke first, to Helen's relief. 'I lost my cool when I saw him there, looking just like those others . . . the ones who . . .' She burst into tears and Helen found herself hugging her.

'Don't,' Helen said presently. 'It's over now—' She recognized her mistake as she spoke.

'But it's not! It's still going on. Killing and killing and killing.'

'And you think it will make things any better if you start up the same kind of feud here?'

'No.' This brought Wendy up short. 'I'm ashamed. I'm truly sorry, Miss Westley. And I'll say so to him, too, if you like.'

'I'm sure he'd be pleased. Mrs Tresikker's taken a fancy to him, so he'll be coming a bit, I hope. Easier if you are speaking to him. I'm just surprised you hadn't met him.' This was another mistake.

'Like calling to like, you mean,' said Wendy. 'You think we're all the same, don't you? All so different from you.'

'I'm sorry.' Now it was Helen's turn to be ashamed. 'You're absolutely right, and I do deeply apologize.'

'Then we're all square,' said Wendy, and went back to her Hoover. 'There's her bell. Tell them I'm sorry. Please?'

'Sure.'

'That's a relief,' said Beatrice. 'I don't think I could stand tribal warfare in the house. Do look, Helen, Peter has brought me the volume of Leonard Woolf's diary. He doesn't seem to have liked poor Paul a bit.' She handed Helen the book.

'And nor did Virginia, by the sound of it. I wonder what was really going on.'

'I think I'd rather not know.' Beatrice closed the subject. 'Mind you treat Wendy gently on the way out, Peter. I think something dreadful happened to her family; I've never dared ask.'

'Something dreadful happened to mine too,' Peter said sombrely. 'But I'm a man of God now, more or less. Don't worry, Mrs Tresikker, we've got a lot in common really, Wendy and I.'

Helen raised the question of new glasses for Beatrice with Hugh Braddock when he dropped in after surgery the next night. 'She can read all right, but her distant vision is terrible,' she told him. 'I hadn't realized until she mentioned it the other day; she just sees us all as blurs. It must be wretched for her. She was showing me her husband's portrait. Have you seen it?'

'No. I had no idea.'

'She used to have it hanging in her bedroom, couldn't face it after she realized he had gone for good. We got it out the other day and she couldn't tell whether the eyes were blue or green. I rather hoped she would keep it out, come to terms with him a bit, but she made me put it away again. Don't mention it, please, she might not like it.' She changed the subject. 'We really do need to think about getting some glasses for her. That nice unpronounceable Peter from St Mary's came up to see her, that's how it came up.'

'I'm glad he came. He's a splendid fellow. How did he and Wendy get on?'

'Quick of you. She opened the door to him and exploded. I hate to think what she was saying to him. But it's OK now. She apologized. She's a honey, that Wendy.'

'She is indeed.'

Something stirred at the back of Helen's mind. 'You've known her for long?'

'Ages. You never know where she is going to turn up next, but I am always pleased when I find her working for one of my patients. She's pure gold, Wendy. Really thinks about people. Look how she went to work and found you for Beatrice.'

'That's quite true; I'd forgotten.'

'Back to Beatrice,' he said. 'Before we can get her to the optician, she's got to be a lot more mobile. Try and persuade her to walk a little more every day. Down the hall and back when she gets up to go to the loo. That sort of thing.'

'She says she can't be bothered. She doesn't want her body strong, if her mind is going. And it's no good pretending that it's not. There are great holes in her memory now, and it upsets her dreadfully when she recognizes one of them.'

'I know. The recent past. And I'm afraid there's no way we can be hopeful about that. Just pray to God and keep her interested and working on the memoir. That really is being a lifeline in every possible sense.'

'Just so long as nothing grisly turns up.'

'What do you mean?'

'I don't know. I just have a feeling.' The bell, rung furiously, interrupted them.

'What are you two conspiring about down there?' Beatrice asked angrily when they joined her. And when Helen explained about the glasses she reacted furiously. 'Why bother working on my wretched body when my mind is going? Walking down the hall! What's the use? Unless we could arrange a strategic fall downstairs?'

'Don't even think about it,' said Hugh. 'You'd probably just break a leg and find yourself immobilized in hospital. The thing you fear most, isn't it?'

'Brute,' she said, but she said it almost cheerfully. 'Don't look so anxious, the two of you,' she went on. 'I'm not sending Helen down to the marsh to pick me a hemlock cocktail. Not yet, anyway. Not while we're busy with the memoir and Jan is due home so soon.'

'Now that is good news.' Hugh Braddock looked at his watch. 'I must be off. No sherry tonight, alas. I've a round to do at the hospital still.'

'They overwork you.' Beatrice was sounding sleepy again.

'Try and get her walking,' Hugh said downstairs as he shrugged into his raincoat. 'But don't worry too much if you can't. Does it matter so much that she only sees us as blurs?'

'I suppose it doesn't really. And it's lovely she is looking forward to Jan coming. Home, she said, did you notice?'

'I most certainly did. That Jan of yours is quite a girl.' He picked up his bag. 'What's all this about hemlock then?'

'Oh dear, I did hope you hadn't noticed.'

'Don't pretend you're stupid. And I'm not either. Of course I noticed. She's been at you too, has she?'

'Yes, right at the start. When she was so wretched. I'm afraid I promised her . . .'

'Idiotic.' He looked at his watch. 'I have to go. Raining again.' And he was gone.

Frances Murray dropped in soon after he had left, and it crossed Helen's mind that she might have hoped to meet him there, as so often on a Friday evening. But she was looking worried, a most unusual thing for her. 'Hang on a mo,' she said as Helen turned to lead the way upstairs. 'I wanted a quick word.'

'Oh?' Helen turned and led the way to the kitchen. 'Yes?'

'It's those Fanshaws, I'm afraid. I do wish I knew just what is going on.'

'What seems to be?'

'I don't know, dammit! They've been to see Finch junior a couple of times. I only discovered this morning when I had to check a back date in his diary. I'd been out both times you see, on a regular weekly date. Well, what I would like to know is whether this is just a coincidence, or if something is going on. Usually we all know a bit about what the others are doing, just enough so we can take over at a pinch. I don't like the feel of this, Helen.'

'No more do I. Oh, there's Beatrice's bell.'

'Damn,' said Frances.

Eleven

'The old witch is at her front window again.' Wendy dropped her jacket on the hall chair. 'Do you think she keeps a diary of our comings and goings?'

'Miss Fanshaw?' Why pretend not to understand? 'Not mine anyway,' Helen went on. 'One of the advantages of having no car is that I walk down by the lanes so I don't pass their house and feel them watching me. Poor things, what a dull life if they've got nothing better to do than sit and keep tabs on their neighbours.' But she must ask Frances if there had been any more visits to Finch & Finch. She was faintly anxious about those.

'How's Beatrice?' Wendy was fetching the Hoover from its cupboard.

'Her memory's worse. Try not to ask her questions, Wendy. It upsets her when she can't get a name.'

'I know. I thought you looked a bit hag-ridden. What does the doctor say?'

'What can he say? But he manages to cheer her up just the same.'

'I'm sure. I'll have a go. She likes to hear about Clive.'

Returning to the breakfast dishes, Helen wondered why Wendy never referred to Hugh Braddock by name. It was always 'the doctor'.

She took advantage of Wendy's presence to go out and

do her shopping, enjoying, as she always did, the friendliness of the little market by the river. Steve the butcher had saved her some kidneys in the fat, because she had mentioned that Beatrice liked them, and they had her favourite kind of yoghurt at the cheese stall.

'How is the old lady?' asked Pat, who ran it.

'Not too bad in herself, but her memory is getting awful.'

'She'd mind that.'

'She does.'

The river was high and the sun shining. Shopping finished, Helen sat for a few minutes on a bench to gaze at the distant view of hills and try not to worry about Beatrice and what the future held for them both. Useless . . . stupid . . . And Jan was coming next week.

In the end, she had to hurry up the steep lanes and arrived, breathless, to find Wendy looking anxious.

'She just rang. I don't know what she wanted. It was horrid. Frightening, a little. She didn't know who I was. She was quite strange . . .'

'Oh dear.' Helen wondered what form the strangeness had taken. 'I'll go right up. Lucky thing, I bought her some violets, she loves them. Off you go, Wendy. I'm sorry, I almost made you late. It was so nice by the river . . .'

'I don't much like to leave you.' But Wendy already had her jacket on. They both knew how tight her timing was. 'Mind you ring the doctor if she doesn't know you either.'

'I certainly will.' Beatrice's bell was ringing. 'She's heard us talking. Mind how you go, Wendy.' She worried sometimes about the speed at which Wendy swept round corners on her high, old-fashioned, unreliable bicycle.

Beatrice was sitting bolt upright in bed, red alarm signals

flying in her cheeks. 'Where have you been? Who's that you were talking to? What's that black woman doing in my house?'

'Beatrice, that's Wendy who cleans for you. You remember, she's got a little boy called Clive.'

'Clive? But he's . . . there's something . . . I don't remember. Helen, you are Helen, aren't you?'

'Indeed I am, and I brought you some violets from the shop in the market, and Steven and Pat both asked how you are.'

'Dying,' said Beatrice. 'But taking too long about it. You are Helen, aren't you, and you promised me—'

'Not that, Beatrice. Not now. Please . . . Jan's coming home next week. You remember Jan, don't you? She was here at Christmas. You liked her; we all did. She's my niece.'

'With a dreadful father,' said Beatrice on a note of triumph. 'Yes, I do remember Jan. We must have a party when she gets here. Smoked salmon, and Hugh, and there's someone else . . .'

'Frances Murray,' Helen told her. 'Your lawyer, remember? And we'll most certainly have a party when Jan gets home. That's a lovely idea.'

'Champagne,' said Beatrice.

Jan was coming on the first Wednesday in April, so Helen planned their little party for the next day, when Wendy would have come to clean. Reminded of it from time to time, Beatrice showed signs of actually looking forward to the party, and Frances had accepted enthusiastically. 'Just what we all need, specially Jan.'

Thinking it over afterwards, Helen was puzzled by this remark, but it was partly explained by a furious telephone call from her brother. He and Marika had confidently expected Jan home for the vacation, despite everything she had said to the contrary, and were only just beginning to take in the fact that she meant to drive straight down to Leyning. 'Her mother was counting on her,' he ended furiously.

'So am I,' said Helen. And then, going to the heart of the matter. 'But not because of the car, Frank. If Marika needs that, of course Jan must leave it with you and come down by train.'

'But Marika hasn't got her licence back. There are all kinds of things she needs to do. And I'm far too busy. You know how it is.'

'I certainly do.' She well remembered the wrench it had been when their mother insisted on selling their little car after becoming bedridden. 'I'm sorry, Frank, I can only suggest you find a good private taxi.'

'Marika finds them so disobliging.' She could well believe this. 'And besides, just between ourselves, we are having to draw in our horns a little. The house sale fell through, very unreasonable fellow, and that hopeless Barnes is taking for ever to sort Mother's will. I imagine that's quite a bore to you too; maybe you should ring up and put some pressure on, Helen. He rather drools about you.'

'Maybe because I *don't* put pressure on. No, we are managing quite nicely down here, and Frances says wills always take for ever to prove.'

'Who the hell is Frances?'

'Sorry. Mrs Tresikker's solicitor. She was a bit doubtful about trying to sell the house so soon.'

'None of her damn business. Or yours. Mind you, your carrying off those two bookcases in that high-handed way was the start of the trouble. Now, you tell Jan from me that she owes it to her mother to come up next week and run her about town for a few days.'

'I'll ask her to phone you, Frank. When she gets here. Now I have to go. Goodbye.'

'Her memory's a bit worse,' she greeted Hugh Braddock when he arrived the next evening. 'Try to cheer her up, Hugh. She's frightened, I think. So am I. It's so sad. Can you stay for a sherry?'

'Make it apple juice. I've got to go on to the hospital.'

'Right. I'll give you ten minutes, then bring it up.'

'The patient's ration! Either not long enough, or too long.' But he said it cheerfully.

'Hugh says I'm a fraud,' Beatrice greeted her when she went up with three glasses on a tray and some bits of cheese for Hugh who was always hungry. 'Just because I know the date of the Battle of Hastings. And 1492. But what use is that, when I don't know whether it's Tuesday or Friday?'

'You do, you know,' Hugh told her. 'I'm here, so it's Friday.'

'And next Thursday we're having Jan's welcome home party,' Helen said. 'Do try and keep that evening clear, Hugh. We're counting on you.'

'I'll do my best. It will be good to see your Jan. She'll cheer us all up. And is Frances coming?'

'Of course. I asked Peter, but he can't, alas.'

'He's a very busy man. And a useful one. And I'm busy too.' He got up. 'Be good, Beatrice. Don't bother to come down and see me out, Helen. I'll drop the key back. You do these stairs quite often enough as it is.'

'Good for me.'

'When did you last go out for a proper walk?'

'I've been gardening,' she said defensively. 'There's a

terrible lot to do still and the weather's been just right for it.'

'But not the same as a walk.' He turned in the doorway. 'If it's too wet underfoot out the back way, you could try downriver past the sewage farm; that lane is tarred.'

'The hemlock used to grow there,' said Beatrice. But Hugh was already running down the stairs and Helen pretended not to hear.

She lay awake a long time that night, anxious thoughts revolving around the problem of Beatrice and that mad promise she had made her. When her own mother had first got ill she had talked a little about the Voluntary Euthanasia Society and a quick, elegant exit. But the more helpless she had become, the more she had seemed to cling to life, and to Helen. Was it just talk with Beatrice too? She did not think so. And she *had* promised. But how did one do it? Who could one ask? She slept at last, fitfully, with nightmares about plastic bags, and smothering pillows, and finally of drowning in a dark and bitter sea that she knew was hemlock.

Jan arrived in a rage. Her father had managed to find out the number of her mobile phone and had rung her when she was doing eighty in heavy traffic on the M25. 'It was damned dangerous.' She dropped her bag on a chair. 'You need all your wits about you on that fast road. I'm sure you didn't give him the number, Helen.'

'Of course I didn't. He probably told a lot of convincing lies; he's good at that. Oh, I'm sorry; I shouldn't have said that. He is your father after all.'

'Unfortunately. How's Beatrice?'

'Looking forward to seeing you. You'd better go right up, Jan dear. She hates it if she thinks we are talking about her down here. Do you mind?'

'Course not. Here, will you put this in the fridge for later, and these in water for me?' She handed Helen a bottle of champagne and a bunch of violets and ran lightly up the stairs.

'Oh dear.' Jan joined Helen in the kitchen ten minutes later. 'She's a lot frailer, isn't she? Her memory is awful, Helen.'

'I know. And so does she, which is the worst of it.'

'Yes. Does she think about dying all the time?'

'A good deal.'

'Part of the time she thought I was you. Helen, have you really promised to help her?'

'Right at the start I did. I don't know what to do.' It was a relief to talk about it.

'Have you talked to Hugh Braddock?'

'Jan, I can't do that. It would involve him, don't you see, and he can't be. Mustn't. They can't do it, doctors, it's against the law, and that oath of theirs. There was one got shopped by a catholic nurse a while ago; had to stand trial. I can't remember whether it was for murder or manslaughter. He got off in the end, but it must have taken years out of his life. Just imagine picking up the pieces after that. So if she is going to be helped, I've got to do it. On my own. I'm sorry she told you, Jan, try to forget it?'

'How can I? What about Frances?'

'She mustn't know either. Think what the Finch brothers would do to her if there was the slightest hint of her being involved. No, it's got to look like an accident, Jan, and I've got to do it, and I wish to God I knew how.'

'Pray for a good ending for her.'

'If I was a praying woman, I would.' High time to change the subject. 'What are you going to do about your parents?'

Jane Aiken Hodge

'Absolutely damn all. I told my father so before I rang off. I've got work to do this vacation, for one thing. I won't be blackmailed for another, and I reckon our first priority is to keep Beatrice cheerful. She's really looking forward to the party tomorrow; she told me all about it. Smoked salmon and champagne. She remembered that. Peter can't come. Who's Peter?'

'A splendid man. He's vicar of the little church out back. Comes in to read to her. It's wonderful she has got such a grip on the idea of the party.'

'Long may it last.'

Jan's coming did Beatrice visible good. She recognized Wendy when she came next morning, and even seemed to realize there might have been something wrong the last time she came.

'She kind of apologized,' Wendy told Helen. 'I nearly cried.'

But next day, Beatrice refused to dress for the party and sit in her big chair. 'I feel safer in bed,' she told Helen. 'And anyway, that way there will be more room for the rest of you.' It was so obviously true that Helen did not waste time and strength in argument. Besides, Beatrice was noticeably less steady on her feet these days. She could still get to the bathroom by herself by clinging to furniture on the way, but it wore her out. Helen had given up all thought of trying to get her to the optician for new glasses. She would just have to go on seeing people as blurs.

'I do hope the party won't be too much for her,' she told Hugh Braddock, who had dropped in before his hospital round, promising to come back later.

'I don't think so. Might do her good; she really seems to be looking forward to it.' He was putting on his shabby

142

windcheater. 'And so am I,' he added surprisingly, and was gone.

Hugh was the last to arrive, late and apologetic, for the party, and Helen was just pouring his champagne when the doorbell rang. 'Who on earth?' She put down the bottle.

'I do hope it's not the Fanshaws,' said Frances.

'I'll get it.' Jan got up from her stool.

She returned in a few minutes, looking both amused and surprised. 'It's the most beautiful young American you ever saw, Beatrice,' she said. 'Asking for you.'

'American? What's her name?'

'His. Ben Norton. Says you're his great-aunt.'

'Good God! Benedicta's grandson?' She reached a shaking hand for her glass and took a strong swig. 'You'd better bring him up, Jan, and another glass.'

'Are you sure, Beatrice?' Helen asked anxiously. 'I do think he might have given you some warning.'

'Never mind. Better like this perhaps? And if he's so beautiful . . . Go on, Jan, fetch him and let's have a look.'

Ben Norton was indeed beautiful, and, Helen thought, he knew it. Everything was handsome about him, from his carefully windswept yellow curls to his designer jeans and trainers. A very expensive young man. And he was charming too. He had Jan in a glow already, and now he was bending over Beatrice making all the right apologies for his surprise appearance in a melodiously mild North American accent. 'And what luck to find you partying with your friends.' His appreciative gaze travelled round the little group and settled on Jan.

It was Helen's cue to pour him champagne and introduce him all round. He refused food. 'I ate at the hotel, didn't want to be a bore. But it took for ever, made me later than I meant – I'm sorry, Aunt Beatrice. May I call you Aunt Beatrice?'

'Of course you may.' She was charmed too, Helen thought. 'But tell me about the family, Ben, I don't know anything. It's been for ever.'

'I know,' he said. 'Nutty. All those years of no speak. So sad, and too late now. That's why I came, see. Last of the line, I am, it's a lonesome feeling. I reckoned you and I might cheer each other up a bit, be family. I could do with some.'

'You mean, Benedicta . . . ?'

'Died a while back. February fill grave. Spunky old bird she was, my granma. Like you, I can see, only maybe not so lucky. Not exactly surrounded by friends at the end. Well, she'd outlived all the family, my pa and ma and both my aunts.'

'And her husband – your grandfather?' Beatrice leaned forward, her eyes fixed on the young man, oblivious to the rest of them.

'Oh, Granpa vamoosed early on. Not a marriage made in heaven that one. Pa was the only child. And as for the Norton millions, they went right back to the Nortons. Lucky thing for Gran that she was pretty well fixed in her own right. She lived like a queen, up there in her Hudson river palace. But we're boring the company,' with an endearingly apologetic smile for the group of fascinated listeners.

'Nonsense,' Beatrice said. 'They're lapping it up, and so am I. You don't get a long-lost great-nephew every day. But if your father was an only child, what do you mean about aunts?'

'Not Pa's sisters, Ma's,' he explained. 'When Pa plucked Ma from the family vine down in Virginia, her two older

144

sisters decided to tag along. Not actually on the honeymoon, I don't think, but pretty damn soon after. I reckon they hoped there might be more where Pa had come from, but if there were, they never got their paws on them. So they settled down to help Ma raise me. And I reckon that's likely why I'm the only one. Pa got kind of busy at work after Lucy and Lavinia moved in. Opened up an office branch in Boston and, funny thing, when he died – quite young – there turned out to be a whole other family up there, large as life and twice as natural. Ma was not pleased. And Granpa was livid.'

'I thought he'd – what was your nice word? – vamoosed?' Beatrice was sitting up straight, sparkling with interest.

'Only to the west coast. He still kept an eye on things – and a close fist on the purse strings. When he finally drank himself to death he had tied things up so tight that not a red cent came our way – nor to the Boston family either, mind you. He'd left the whole kit and caboodle to the Republican Party, would you believe it? Granma seethed. Said it was all my fault, but I never could see why. But then, sweet reason was never Granma's line so you would notice. You must remember that, surely, even after all the years.'

'I sure do.' Helen noticed with amusement that Beatrice's speech had modified slightly towards American. 'But, poor Benedicta, do you really mean to tell me that sad sack Dick Norton walked out on her? I didn't think much of him the one time I met him, that's for sure, but that's no way for a Norton to behave.'

'That's what everyone said, which can't have made it any easier for poor old Gran. Not that she was poor old Gran, mind you. From all I've heard she was the world's dizziest grass widow. Cut quite a swathe did my granma in her day. When she realized that Granpa was gone for good she shut up the Norton house in Boston, moved back to that gothic palace on the upper Hudson and turned her life into one long weekend.'

'Oh, poor Ben,' said Beatrice.

'Not a bit of it. Very rich Ben, she was. Nobody knows what she got out of Norton at the time he left, but it was plenty, and then when the old man died – your father – of course she was richer still. That's when she moved to New York to that penthouse flat of his, and started really living it up. Pearl Harbor sobered her up a bit, but she found something pretty glitzy that she called war work, rushing to and fro between New York and Washington, holding important hands. "Best years of my life", she used to say. She talked to me a lot when I was a kid. I used to get sent there for vacations when Ma and the aunts were travelling. They went on husband-hunting to their dying day, my aunts Lucy and Lavinia.'

'You stayed with Benedicta in New York?' Beatrice was beginning to tire, Helen thought. Her words were slurring a little.

'Oh, no, worse luck. That would have been something. No, she'd sold up in New York by the time I was into my teens, after she had her first little stroke. She was back in the Hudson river castle, with a whole train of servants and some interesting company.'

'I think that's enough for now.' Hugh Braddock came across from his chair in the corner to pick up Beatrice's hand and check her pulse. 'Time we all went home and left Mrs Tresikker in peace.'

'I'm sure you're right.' Helen joined him by the bed, relieved at the intervention.

'Sleepy,' said Beatrice, lying back. 'Come again in the morning, Paul. Glad you came.'

Downstairs, Hugh looked at his watch. 'I must be on my way. There's someone I need to check on at the hospital. Can I give you a lift?' he asked Ben Norton. 'If it's the Black Swan it's on my way.'

'Thanks, yes. Terrible place; service like treacle and stinks of old gravy. Kind of you, it's further than I thought. Unless I can give a hand with the clearing up?' With a hopeful look at Helen. 'I'm quite house-trained.'

'Thanks.' Helen could see that he wanted to stay, but felt oddly reluctant to have him. 'But we tend to leave it till the morning. Come for a drink before lunch? I know Beatrice will wake up asking for you. Stay for soup and a sandwich? I'm afraid we live a pretty quiet life; she has to take things very easily, but she will want to make the most of you while you are here. Trouble is, she tires so quickly.'

'Yes.' Hugh had donned his shabby mackintosh. 'Sorry I broke it up back there, but that was long enough. And you're right about tomorrow, Helen. Lunch downstairs, and keep an eye on things.'

'Right.' She was glad of the support.

'Great.' Ben pulled on a sky-blue windcheater. 'Twelve o'clock suit you? Anything I can fetch for you on the way over? It looks a great little town, Leyning. I'm looking forward to exploring it.' He held the front door solicitously for Hugh, as for an old person, smiled brilliantly and impartially at the three of them, and was gone.

'That was a fine upstanding lie of yours.' Frances Murray rolled up her sleeves and began washing glasses. 'Why didn't you want him to stay on, Helen?'

'I don't know, can't think. I just knew I didn't.'

'Beatrice is fast asleep.' Jan joined them with a tray of plates and glasses. 'I turned the light out. That wasn't very friendly of you, Helen, turning the poor boy out in the cold at what must seem like the beginning of the evening to him.'

'I know. I feel a pig now.'

'Did you notice that Beatrice called him Paul?' asked Jan.

'Yes, wasn't it odd? I suppose all that talk of the old days made her think of her husband.'

'What a tale,' said Frances. 'Not a very nice family by the sound of them.'

'But he's a proper charmer,' said Jan.

'Isn't he just? And doesn't he know it?'

'That's not fair, Helen,' Jan protested. 'He was only trying to make himself agreeable to a bunch of surprise strangers. He must have expected to find Beatrice all on her own, like his grandmother.'

'Sounded sad, didn't it?' said Frances. 'All by herself in that huge house. Well, that's done.' She emptied the washing-up bowl, took off her apron and rolled down her sleeves. 'I must be on my way. Thanks for a surprising party, Helen. I do hope Beatrice is none the worse in the morning. I'll give you a ring from the office. Don't get up, you look knackered.' Helen had subsided on to a kitchen stool. 'Jan will see me out. Lovely evening. See you soon.'

Twelve

'I slept right through,' Beatrice boasted in the morning. 'And dreamed of Paul. Good dreams.' She smiled, remembering. 'Can I have a boiled egg? I'm hungry! And, Helen, I didn't dream that young man, did I? Benedicta's grandson?'

'No, indeed. Ben Norton. He's coming for a drink at twelve, staying for a sandwich lunch. Downstairs, doctor's orders. But you shall have him to yourself first.'

'A sandwich? Hardly a fatted calf.'

'Hardly a prodigal.'

'No, I suppose not. But make them special sandwiches, Helen. He was fun, wasn't he? I liked him, didn't I?'

'Very much, I thought. We all did.' It was the least she could say. 'I'll see that they are the very best prodigal's sandwiches. And you are going to get up and dress for him, aren't you?'

'I suppose so. I keep thinking about Benedicta, Helen. Dying all by herself in that great, glum house with no one about her but servants. I woke up this morning thinking how lucky I am. "Partying with my friends." Nice phrase, wasn't it?'

'Very. He has a gift for nice phrases, your great-nephew.'

'Like Paul. Fancy me having a great-nephew. Helen, there's something I need to do this morning. I thought of it

149

in the night. Now, what was it?' She began to twist her hands in the bedspread, always a bad sign.

'Don't fret for it,' Helen advised. 'It'll come back when you've had your breakfast. One egg coming up right away.'

Ben Norton arrived sharp at twelve, bearing an enormous mixed bouquet. 'For my favourite great-aunt.' He handed the dripping flowers to Jan, who had let him in. 'How is she this morning? Not too zonked by last night, I hope.'

'No, she's fine. Looking forward to seeing you. Helen's up with her; why don't you go right on up while I put these in water.'

'Thanks.' He hung the blue windcheater on a hook, glanced in the hall mirror to check windswept curls and loped down the hall to the stairs.

'Look at you, up and dressed.' Helen thought for a moment that he was going to kiss Beatrice, but he must have decided against it. 'I brought you some flowers, Aunt Beatrice; that nice Jan of yours is putting them in water for me. I hope you like them.'

'I'm sure I shall. Now tell me all about yourself.'

'There's a stopper of a question.' He pulled a comic, self-deprecating face, and Helen thought it her cue to leave them alone.

Returning with Beatrice's tray soon after one, she found them deep in conversation.

'Not lunch already?' Beatrice protested. 'We're only getting started on Ben's life. He ran away from school three times, Helen, and would you believe it, they sent him back each time.'

'I'm surprised the school would have him,' said Helen.

'Oh, Nortons have been going to Phillips Exeter ever since the school was founded,' Beatrice explained.

'And remembering it in their wills,' said Ben, rising to move a little table conveniently close to Beatrice's chair. 'They took me back all right, but they didn't love me much. Lunch for one, I see, just like the doctor ordered. Eat your soup while it's hot, Aunt Beatrice, and may I come back afterwards?'

'I'm afraid probably not,' said Helen, on the stairs. 'She usually sleeps for an hour or so after lunch. We're having ours in the kitchen, I hope you don't mind.'

'Super kitchen,' he said, looking round. 'Nicest room in the house, if it's nice at all. What happens beyond your garden wall?' He was peering out the window over the sink.

'A little church and then open country,' Helen told him, ladling soup into bowls.

'Just the very thing I need. Come for a walk after lunch, Jan, and see I don't get lost in your wild country-side?'

'Good idea.' Helen took her place at the kitchen table. 'Peter says the blackthorn is still full out in the graveyard, Jan. Time you got out there. And bring Ben back for a cup of tea. Beatrice is bound to wake up full of questions she has forgotten to ask you.' To Ben.

'Or forgotten the answers,' he said.

'You've noticed?'

'Sure I have. Sticks out a mile, doesn't it, poor old duck. Bothers her. There's something really bugging her right now; something she wants to do. Can't think what it is.'

'I know,' said Helen. 'It does happen, I'm afraid. I find the best thing is to try not to let her fret about it, and then it usually comes back.'

'Or she forgets all about it and starts worrying about

something else? Granma was like that towards the end, but she was a hell of a lot vaguer than Aunt Beatrice, I can tell you. Trouble was, most of the time she only had servants to talk to, and she didn't reckon much to them, so she let herself go, kind of; slid away, worse every time I visited. Vaguer, you know, not really on the ball. Sad to see. I don't suppose for a minute Aunt Beatrice realizes how lucky she is to have all of you. Talking to her. Caring about her. Keeping her going.'

'We're lucky too,' Jan told him. 'She's our asylum.'

'Odd word to pick, surely?'

'No, it's the right one. We were homeless, Helen and I, when she took us in.'

'Yes.' Helen had wanted the chance to say this. 'I feel a bit bad about that. It seems awful not to ask you to stay, Ben, but the upstairs spare room is chock-a-block with all our stuff.'

'The turret room? I'd love to see that. It was where he worked, wasn't it? The lost poet?'

'Why do you call him that?'

'Granma always did. Hey, the sun's out. How about it, Jan?' He had been eating with ferocious speed, now pushed his chair back. 'Promise to leave the dishes for when we get back, Helen. I'm a dab hand at a sink.'

'I'll put some boots on.' Jan finished a last bite of prawn sandwich. 'Will you be all right in trainers, Ben? It's pretty muddy out there.'

'Sure; they wash. No problem. I can't wait to see what's on the other side of that wall.'

'We felt just the same,' Helen told him. 'Only it took us longer.'

'I hate to waste time.' He was stacking his and Jan's dishes expertly in the sink.

'I can see you do,' she told him wryly. A slow eater, she was still only halfway through her sandwich and had meant to eat an apple afterwards.

When she went up to fetch Beatrice's tray she found her back in bed and fast asleep, as she had expected. She was just finishing the dishes when the telephone rang and she hurried to answer it before it woke Beatrice.

'Frances? I thought it would be you.'

'I've been waiting for a good moment to call.' Helen knew this meant that the three Finches had gone out for one of their leisurely working lunches. 'How's Beatrice? None the worse, I hope?'

'No. Had a wonderful night, been hearing the story of Ben's life this morning and snug asleep now.'

'That's good news. I was worried a bit, back there.'

'Oh, so was I; glad when Hugh broke it up.'

'You're free to talk? Where's the handsome stranger now?'

'Gone out for a walk with Jan. Frances, am I a pig for not inviting him to stay?'

'Not a bit of it, and the more he hints the less you should do it. You've got quite enough on your hands as it is, without a hungry young male to feed. And besides, if he'd wanted to be welcomed like a long-lost kinsman he should have behaved like one and let you know in advance. Or Beatrice rather.'

'Yes, that's rather the way I feel. Honestly, Frances, I didn't much fancy the way he took it for granted he could charm his way in.'

'I couldn't agree with you more. But it worked all right on Beatrice.'

'And on Jan, but then she's his age.'

'Younger,' said Frances. 'I bet that young Adonis is

nearer thirty than twenty, and what's he been doing all his life, that's what I'd like to know. And what's he doing now, come to that, so he can come roaring across the Atlantic to visit an unknown great-aunt?'

'Oh,' said Helen. 'I hadn't thought of that. But I suppose he's so rich that he doesn't have to work.'

'Everyone ought to work,' said Frances.

'You're so fierce. But of course I agree with you. Mind you, we don't in the least know that he doesn't.'

'He doesn't seem like one of the world's toilers.'

'No. So what are we going to do about him?'

'Wait and see. Nothing rash. Let Beatrice enjoy him. So long as she is?'

'Oh, enormously. He's doing her good. She's dressed today.'

'Well, there you are. Just don't let him wear her out.'

'No indeed, though mind you, Frances, we know that given the choice she'd rather wear out than rust out.'

'Of course she would. Oh damn, I must go.'

'Goodbye.' Helen put down the receiver with a vision of Finches on the prowl.

Jan and Ben returned from their walk quite late, very muddy and extremely cheerful.

'It's super, your English countryside,' Ben told Helen. 'May I take these off right here and go sock foot? They're filthy.'

'Not the socks, I'm glad to see!' They were a remarkable psychedelic blue.

'No, ma'am. I'm a seasoned traveller from all those times with Ma and the aunts. I wash them every night, clean on in the morning.'

'Not the same ones?'

'Sure. Saves luggage. A bit damp this morning, but never mind.'

'I thought your mother and aunts always left you behind with your grandmother.' Jan had taken off her boots and changed into slippers.

'Not when I got older they didn't. I turned into an asset overnight when my voice broke. Is the old darling awake yet?' To Helen.

'Yes, and asking for you. She's had her tea, would you like a cup?'

'No, thanks, never touch the stuff.'

'Fruit juice then?'

'No, thanks. A glass of water maybe?' He reached one down from the cupboard and turned on the tap.

'He hoped for something stronger,' said Jan when he had gone upstairs.

'He should be so lucky!'

'You're so tough. I'm sorry we were late, Helen. I couldn't get him to turn back, he was enjoying himself so. Did Beatrice mind?'

'A bit. Partly because she's tired; I'm not going to let him stay long tonight. Has he said anything about how long he's here for, by the way? It makes a difference, doesn't it?'

'I suppose so. No, not a word. He's never been to Europe before; talked about France and Spain a bit, as if he thought of going there, but nothing about dates. Do you think we ought to clear out the turret room and ask him to stay, Helen?'

'I'd wondered, but Frances says no, and I think I agree with her.'

'Frances has a lot of sense. She telephoned, did she?'

'Yes, I told her Beatrice is fine this morning. Oh, there's her bell. No, I'll go, thanks.'

'I've thought of it!' Beatrice was sitting upright in her chair looking pleased with herself. 'I need to see Frances. Could you ring her for me, Helen? Ask her if she could drop in on her way home from work.'

'Of course. I'll do it right away.' She thought for a moment of going to the downstairs telephone, but changed her mind and picked up the receiver by the bed to dial the familiar office number. Through to Frances, she got an instant assent.

'Of course. I'm about done here. I'll be along as soon after six as I can make it. Give her my love.'

'All fixed.' Helen put down the receiver and smiled at Beatrice. 'Soon after six.'

'Then I'd better be getting along.' Ben pleased Helen by rising to his feet. 'Let you have a bit of a rest before the lawyer lady comes, Aunt Beatrice. I've persuaded Jan to show me the town tonight, and she tells me they have some kind of a local farmers' shindig by the river tomorrow, so we're planning to go to that. OK if I drop in afterwards? Twelvish?' To Helen.

'Do, if you can face soup and a sandwich again.' What else could she say?

Frances arrived, briefcase in hand, soon after Ben had left. 'Do I take it that this is a business meeting?' she asked Helen at the front door.

'I think so. It will be her will, won't it, now Ben has turned up.'

'That's what I thought. Shall I go right up?'

'Do. And shout when you are ready for a glass of something. Jan's showing Ben the town tonight.'

'Yes. I saw them striding off across the river. He's going to find it pretty small-time, I'd think.'

156

'Me too. Stay to supper, Frances, it's lazy woman's food, no problem.'

'Thanks, I'd like to.' She vanished up the stairs.

'Well, that's done.' Frances joined Helen in the kitchen twenty minutes later. 'And being Beatrice she wants it signed and sealed as soon as possible, if not sooner. Tell me, Helen, what sort of terms are you on with the Fanshaw ladies these days?'

'I suppose you'd call it armed neutrality. They don't quite cut me in the street but they look as if they'd like to. Oh dear, does she want them as witnesses again?'

'Sensible really, if we can fix it.'

'I suppose so.' She pulled a face. 'And you can bet your boots they'll come if asked. They are bound to have noticed Ben coming and going, must be dying to know all about him. So, who's going to bell the cats, you or me?'

'Best from you, don't you think? I've promised Beatrice I'll go in and get it typed up first thing in the morning. Nice peaceful Saturday. So if you could ask them to come in later on?'

'Ben is coming to see Beatrice about twelve.'

'Before that then. Get it done with?'

'Right.' She picked up the receiver and dialled.

As usual, it was Ellen who answered. 'Tomorrow?' She sounded appalled. 'Saturday? But it's the farmers' market. We never miss that, Susan and I. Such bargains, you know, we can't afford to miss them with the cost of living going up every day under this dreadful government.' She was talking, Helen thought, to give herself time to fight the battle between umbrage and curiosity.

'You couldn't go early?' she coaxed. 'Come here at about eleven? Thing is, Mrs Tresikker has a young relative from the States in town at the moment, he's coming to see her at twelve. Frances Murray wants to get it all done before then.'

'Oh, I see. A young relative, you say? How lovely for her . . .'

'Yes, a great-nephew she didn't even know existed. It has cheered her up in the most remarkable way.'

'No need for Dr Braddock, you mean? Tomorrow?'

'Do you know, I actually hadn't thought of that. Thank you for reminding me. I'd better give him a ring, hadn't I?'

'I'm surprised Frances Murray didn't.' Delighted with herself, Ellen yielded almost gracefully. 'Very well, Susan and I will just set the alarm early and get to the market when it opens. That should get us over to you comfortably by eleven.'

'That's wonderful, thank you.' Helen hung up and smiled at Frances. 'Triumph of curiosity over huffiness,' she told her. 'Coming at eleven. And should we ask Hugh Braddock? She suggested it, actually.'

'I thought that must be it. Just ring and tell him, Helen. I don't really think we need him for this little bit of work, and he is such a busy man.'

'I know. He's looking exhausted. I could kill that housekeeper of his.' She looked at her watch. 'I'll ring him right away, bit of luck he'll be home for his supper, such as it is.' She dialled, got Hugh at once and put the question, then turned to Frances. 'He's got a committee meeting,' she said. 'Asks if you think he ought to cut it.'

'No,' said Frances at once. 'Tell him it's no big deal.'

'We can always get him on his mobile,' said Helen after she had passed on the message and rung off.

'If the Fanshaws rile her too dreadfully,' Frances agreed.

* * *

158

This time everything went smoothly. Frances and the Miss Fanshaws all arrived together soon after eleven o'clock and it was all done before half past. Back downstairs, Miss Ellen looked hopefully about the hall where Helen was waiting with their coats.

'But where is the beautiful great-nephew?' she asked. 'Mrs Tresikker looks a different creature. You must be delighted he is doing her so much good.' There was something in her tone that Helen did not altogether like.

'Yes, it's wonderful, she's thriving on him. You didn't see them at the farmers' market?' she asked. 'He's there with my niece, Jan. She's been showing him the town a bit.'

'Kind of her.' Once again there was something in Ellen Fanshaw's tone that Helen neither liked nor understood. She looked at her watch; she really ought to offer the sisters a neighbourly cup of coffee, but Frances was already helping them into their coats, and Beatrice's bell was ringing upstairs. She was finding it more and more difficult to get herself to the loo, and Helen hurried upstairs to help her.

Safe back in bed, Beatrice grinned at Helen. 'Such a surprise for him,' she said. 'Just what he needs. But not a word, Helen, it is to be a surprise. And no, I'm not going to get dressed today. I do find those Fanshaws quite tiring. But that was funny too,' she said with another wicked grin. 'I think I'll have just a little nap before Ben gets here.' She snuggled comfortably down under the duvet. 'Bless you and thank you, Helen dear, for being so good to me.' And she closed her eyes for instant sleep.

Frances was waiting in the downstairs hall. 'I wanted a word, Helen. Is Beatrice OK?'

'Fine, but tired, having a little sleep before Ben gets here.

Very pleased with herself, actually. She said the nicest thing to me. Let's be ladies, shall we, and sit in the front room? Jan and Wendy have made it so nice between them. What's on your mind?' she asked, as they settled on the sofa that faced the front window.

'I've a confession to make,' Frances began, and then, 'Oh, hell!' They had both heard the sound of voices on the steps and then Jan's key in the lock. 'Helen, no private session today, please. Make it sociable, don't leave Ben alone with her?' Frances broke off as Jan put her head round the door.

'There you are,' Jan said. Something was wrong with her today. 'We'd have been here sooner only we ran into the Fanshaws. Dying to meet Ben, they were. Knew all about him. Full of nods and winks and significant looks.'

'Oh dear,' said Helen. 'And Beatrice wanted it to be a surprise. Ben's not gone up, I hope? She's having a little sleep.'

'No, he's in the downstairs loo, making himself beautiful for her.' There was something very odd in her tone.

Frances had noticed it too. 'How was the farmers' market?'

'Crowded as usual. But I found Beatrice some of that honey soap she likes. Ben had forgotten his wallet, so it was spectating only for him.'

'Aren't I an idiot?' Ben joined them, every golden curl in place. 'I can see it now, sitting on the shelf back at the hotel. I meant to pick it up last thing but I was in a rush, afraid of keeping Jan waiting by the cold river. Lucky you Brits are such an honest lot. Pity though, I wanted to buy Aunt Beatrice some more flowers. OK to go up to her, Helen? I thought I'd best ask in case those two witches had worn her out.'

'Leave it for a bit, Ben. She said she'd have a little nap.' She caught Frances' eye. 'And then I thought we might all have a glass of champagne, seeing as it is Saturday. You'll stay, Frances, won't you?'

'Love to. Thanks.'

'A celebration,' said Ben. 'Super.'

'I'll put a bottle in the fridge.' Jan slid from the room. What was wrong with Jan?

Thirteen

'Partying again, such joy.' Ben raised his glass. 'Here's to you, Aunt Beatrice, and all your lovely friends. How I wish Granma could see us now, so happy here. Why was she always so mean about you, Aunt Beatrice? Because you were so much the brightest, or because you saw the lost poet first? I've been dying to ask, and you can't beat good old alcohol for Dutch courage.' He sipped champagne and went on. 'Honest and true, Aunt B, it seemed so odd the way he hung around there all the time, talking on and on about that great philosophical poem of his and not writing it. No wonder old Granma got sick of it in the end and threw him out. I wish I'd been there to see. But he must have told you all about it when he got back. I've been longing to ask, didn't have the nerve.'

There was a cold little silence. Then, 'I don't know what you are talking about,' Beatrice said. 'You surely never met my husband.'

'No, ma'am. Granma saw to that. No way was I wanted when he was hanging about, "recharging his batteries" in her lovely company. But she told me all about it afterwards. And I helped with the bonfire.'

'Bonfire?' Beatrice's hands were working at her quilt. I must stop this, Helen thought. But how? Ben was going right on.

162

'That last time he came, the time she threw him out, he'd brought his collected works with him in an old black canvas bag. Ma and the aunts were off in Bermuda that Christmas, I remember it well. Years ago, I was just a kid, but I'll never forget that bonfire. We had it out in the snow, the day I got there. She'd been waiting for me, see. Bonfires were hardly her line, poor old duck. And the bag stank, burning, and she said, "Thus perish all traitors!" I thought about it a lot, afterwards. Thought I ought to tell someone, never could think who. Then, when I heard you were all on your own here I decided it had to be you. I hope I did right.' He was becoming aware of the stillness around him.

Beatrice's hands clenched on the quilt. 'Of course you did right,' she told him. 'I needed to know. Just think of it! All those years. To and fro. "Recharging his batteries." Here and there. Her and me, and his great work. And you helped her burn the lot! Oh, that's funny, that's a real joke. Helen, are you there? I can't see you properly. It is funny, isn't it? The joke's on all of us. But especially on you!' To Ben. And then, 'Helen, where are you? I am laughing, aren't I?'

'Yes, darling, of course you are laughing.' Helen had her arms round her, holding her up, feeling her shake. 'Gently now, gently . . .' She felt Beatrice stiffen in her arms, then relax, heavy against her.

Frances was there, helping. 'She's gone.' Together they laid Beatrice softly down. 'Jan, ring Hugh. Tell him. And you,' to Ben. 'Get out of this house. Now.'

'But—'

'Just go,' she said, and he went.

'Hugh's coming.' Jan put the receiver down. 'Is she really . . . ?'

'Yes. I think we've just seen murder done.' Frances had

watched the door close behind Ben Norton. 'My fault. I should have stopped him.'

'But, Frances.' Helen was beginning to take it in. 'I won't believe it. He can't have done it on purpose. Can he? And if he did –' she thought about it – 'it was what she wanted after all . . .' She reached a gentle hand to close the staring eyes. ' "Partying with her friends." But, surely, Frances, he was just stupid, not wicked?'

'Wicked as hell. It's what he came to do. That's what I've been trying to tell you. Didn't get the chance. I didn't like the feel of things the other night, when he turned up. I put a call through to a friend in Boston. Asked him to check up on young Ben Norton. Roger came back to me this morning at the office when I was getting that codicil typed up. He's got a record a mile long, that young charmer. Cut off by the family long ago. Out on his uppers. Took a chance on charming his way in here with an eye on Beatrice's estate.'

'Horrible,' said Helen, beginning to believe. 'But how did he know?'

'He *is* horrible,' Jan broke in. 'I've got a tale to tell too. But not now, not here. Poor Beatrice . . .'

'Not poor Beatrice,' said Helen. 'We're not going to think like that. She'd enjoyed having him so much, right up to the last moment. She'd come alive for him.'

'And the joke was on him,' said Frances. 'And she saw it, bless her. She really was laughing. What a woman.'

'Oh?' Helen did not understand.

'I really don't see why I shouldn't tell you. That codicil she signed this morning. He took it for granted she'd left him everything, didn't he? Saw himself as the obvious heir and wasted no time. Well, there was no time to waste. His past was bound to catch up with him soon enough. But what Beatrice actually left him was her husband's papers and permission to write about him. She thought it was what he needed, something to do. He reminded her of Paul, she said. It was right Ben should do it; he would understand him. And he had helped Benedicta burn the lot. The joke really was on both of them, wasn't it?'

'Not all that funny.' Helen looked down at the still figure on the bed. 'What will Ben Norton do now, do you think?'

'Get out of town smartish, I imagine, but wait about close by, expecting to hear something to his advantage.'

'He'll get out all right,' said Jan. 'I haven't had a chance to tell you what happened last night. Not here . . .' She was making heroic efforts not to cry.

'No, downstairs, while we wait for Hugh.' Helen straightened the duvet with gentle hands while Frances and Jan quietly picked up the bottle and glasses.

'So, what is it, Jan?' Helen asked. Nobody had even thought of another drink and they were perched miserably on kitchen chairs, in what felt like suspended animation. 'What happened last night? I didn't hear you come in.'

'No, I was.late. I went for a walk by the river, afterwards, trying to decide what I should do. I couldn't think straight. Well, obviously I couldn't or I wouldn't have let any of this happen.' Jan was crying now, but quietly, tears of relief. 'It's all my fault. I should have told you right away, this morning, but he begged me not to, said it would spoil everything with Beatrice. She was the first bit of loving family he had ever had, he said. Told a terrible tale of his childhood; said sometimes he just couldn't help himself, lost control. Flipped.

'Everything went wrong last night, you see. He'd wanted to take me out to the Leyning Bistro, but they don't take

165

American Express cards, he said, so we ate at the Black Swan and it was pretty gruesome. He was feeling bad about that, and I was trying to cheer him up, so when he suggested we go up to his room to fetch his jacket before he walked me home I never thought twice about it.'

'Oh my God,' said Frances. 'What happened, Jan?'

'Horrible. He just took it for granted he was going to have me there and then, wasting no time, on the floor. Thought that was what I had come for. When I tried to stop him, he went mad – literally. He changed. his eyes changed colour; it was terrifying. He's strong, too.'

'What did you do?' Helen was almost afraid to ask.

'Screamed like a steam engine. I didn't know I could do it, but I did. And he let me go, and said sorry, and his eyes changed back to blue again, and someone came knocking on the door and I told them it was nothing, just a fright. And Ben was on his knees, grovelling, begging me to say nothing; to meet him in the morning, let him explain. He kept saying about Beatrice, how it would upset her, and of course it was true, she was enjoying him so. He was doing her such good. So in the end I agreed to meet him this morning, and came away and walked and walked and walked, wondering if I was right not to tell you at once. So then, of course, I overslept, and rushed out to meet him and he told me this terrible tale about a wretched child-hood, parents who hated him, kept on sending him back to a school he loathed. He got these violent fits, he said, couldn't help himself. All he wanted was not to upset Beatrice, begged me to let him have one last happy meeting with her and then he'd go, leave her with good memories. And I believed him. Idiot . . . fool . . .'

'He fooled us all,' said Frances. 'A practised hand. I'm just grateful it was no worse, Jan. That you had the wits to scream. His record's terrible. Ah.' The front door bell had rung. 'That'll be Hugh at last.'

'Just what I expected.' Hugh joined them in the kitchen. 'And what she wanted. We must remember that. I do see, Helen, that what that young ruffian did almost certainly precipitated it, but it was going to happen anyway, and she'd be the first to say he did her a kindness. Let it go . . . let him go. He'll be his own disaster in the end. In fact, he's in trouble already. I was called out to the Black Swan first thing this morning. There had been some kind of a ruckus there last night and an elderly visitor had suffered what she claimed was a heart attack. Indigestion, if you ask me, but that's neither here nor there. Anyway, when I came away there was a panic on at the desk. Young Norton had eaten a hearty breakfast and vanished. Nothing in his room; he only had a rucksack apparently. He must have got it out when they were busy with my patient.'

'He told me he made a point of travelling light,' Helen said. 'Now I see why. But what a fool, scarpering like that. How does he think he's going to be able to turn up and claim the estate he expects to inherit?'

'I reckon he had no choice,' said Jan. 'I think he was skint. He always managed not to pay for things. I'm such a fool. I should have noticed. Those flowers he brought Beatrice. They were dripping, no wrapping paper. He must have stolen them from the florist in the market. I thought it was funny at the time, forgot all about it.'

'All his credit cards had been stopped some time ago,' put in Frances, rising. 'I'd better get in touch with the police. Put them in the picture. Pity the Black Swan didn't ring here when he vanished, but I suppose he had said nothing about Beatrice. Nasty, careful young man. I'll be in the office, Helen dear, let me know if there is anything I can do. All right to go ahead with arranging the funeral, Hugh?'

'Of course. Do you know what she wanted?'

'The least possible trouble for anyone, she told me. She didn't reckon much to bodies. Didn't want to be a nuisance. But that was back at New Year's, before she knew us, when she was all alone.'

'And now we want to take trouble for her,' Helen said. 'Celebrate her. But how?'

Peter provided the answer to this, calling late that afternoon, soon after the undertaker's men had driven away leaving the house an empty shell.

'I am so sorry.' He took and held both of Helen's hands. 'I came as soon as I could. We both know it is what she wanted, but that won't stop us missing her.'

'Dreadfully.' It did her good to say it. 'I'm all at sea.'

'Bound to be, for a while. Just take it as it comes. And I promise you, you will feel better after the funeral. And that is what I came to talk about.'

'Oh?' Surprised.

'She didn't tell you? I did wonder. She told me she would like to be buried in my graveyard, among the snowdrops. I promised her a good, plain funeral without what she called any religious nonsense. Will you trust me for it?'

'Of course I will. I'm so relieved. Just over the garden wall, and then we can all come back and have a wake for her here. Oh I am so grateful, Peter. It makes it seem almost easy.'

'She told me she liked the idea of being buried. Said she hadn't been much use in the world, but at least she would grow a few more snowdrops. A cardboard coffin, she wanted.'

'Oh.' She had let the kind undertaker talk her into expensive mahogany.

'I'll tell them, don't worry.' He had read her mind. 'I could do it Wednesday afternoon; over before Easter.'

'Oh, thank you.' She had been worrying about this too. So much to worry about.

'I loved her,' he said.

'So did I. So did we all. She was worrying about not being useful, but I don't know what I am going to do without her.'

He looked at her very kindly and she was afraid he was going to tell her to leave it to God. But instead he just said, 'Take it a day at a time.'

Wendy appeared later that evening, fresh from work, with Clive on the carrier of her bicycle.

'I can't stop,' she greeted Helen. 'Peter told me. I'm so sad and so glad for her that I don't know what to do. And I came to say shall I come Wednesday instead of Thursday and help you get straight for the funeral?'

'Oh, thank you, Wendy. And come back afterwards, help with the wake?'

'I'd like that. Can I bring Clive? You'll likely get quite a few people. She was loved.'

'She had heard pretty fast.' Jan had been in the kitchen, making soup.

'Yes. Peter told her.'

'Oh.' And then, 'Helen, you look all in. The soup's almost ready. Early supper, don't you think, and bed? Things will look better in the morning.'

'I certainly hope so.' Deeply worried about Jan, she had hoped that making supper would do her good.

They ate it almost in silence. At last, Jan looked up from rinsing out the sink. 'Helen, I feel so awful. Such a coward! If I'd only spoken up last night, or even this morning, none of this would have happened.'

'But how were you to know?' Helen had expected this. 'And Beatrice was enjoying him so much. I can see how you didn't want to spoil it for her. After all, being a rapist doesn't necessarily make a man a murderer. And do remember, Jan, that he did Beatrice a kindness, really. And me too, come to that.'

'You? A kindness? What on earth do you mean?'

'You've not been here since New Year's. She was getting steadily worse, and she knew it. She was beginning to talk more and more about sending me down to the marsh for a bunch of hemlock for her. A final draught. She was putting pressure on Hugh, too, I think, when she saw him alone, though of course he never said anything. But I'm sure that's why he has been coming so often. He was afraid of what she might get me to do.'

'And Ben did it for her. For his own wicked reasons. How very strange.' She thought about it. Then, 'Thank you, Helen, that is going to help, I think. What a brave woman. Would you have done it for her in the end, do you think?'

'Jan, I don't know. But I have to say that I do feel some relief mixed up in all the sadness. Not to have to think of her any more, straining for memory, struggling to the loo by herself and pretending it didn't hurt.'

'You should have told me how bad it was getting.'

'You'd have seen soon enough. I'm so glad you are here, Jan.'

'Me, too,' said Jan.

In bed at last, Helen lay awake for a long time worrying
about Jan, and then, when sleep was just beginning to
hover, she started to worry about herself. It was so strange
not to be listening for Beatrice's bell. And what was she
going to do without her? Shaming to be thinking financial
thoughts, but impossible not to. It had become increasingly
difficult to get Beatrice to sign cheques lately, and more and
more she had shirked the battle and simply paid the bills
herself. A recent statement from her own bank had given
her a fright and she had promised herself that she would
sort things with Beatrice, but the chance had never come.
She was back where she had started from, homeless and
almost penniless. Disgusting to be thinking like this. She
fell asleep at last, late and heavily, and was wakened by the
telephone and Jan's voice answering it. Amazingly, the
clock by her bed said half past nine.

'Stay right where you are.' Jan put her head round the
door. 'You're going to have breakfast in bed, like it or not.
That was Frances. She sends her love and says everything is
under control for Wednesday and you are just to take it
easy today. Not much else we can do actually, being Sunday. We thought we'd go for a walk this afternoon and I
asked her back to supper. I hope that's OK?'

'Lovely,' she said, ate her breakfast and fell fast asleep
again.

She felt better when she next woke and saw that it was
nearly twelve o'clock. Dressing rapidly she went down and
found Jan in the kitchen, reading cook books.

'I'm cooking supper tonight,' she announced, 'and you
are going to do nothing all day. Doctor's orders. He
dropped in early on and told me to cherish you. And feed
you up. So how about one of my omelettes for lunch?'

'Lovely.' Helen felt absurdly cross. Why? Because Jan

and Frances had not suggested she join them on their walk, or because she had missed Hugh's visit? Or just because her occupation was gone and she was tired to death? Wretched phrase. 'I wish they had left her here,' she said suddenly. 'It doesn't feel right, not having her up there.'

'I know. I keep expecting to hear her bell.'

'Should we do something about starting on her room?'

'Not today. Hugh said do nothing, and Frances said don't worry.'

'Idiotic,' said Helen. But it was good to sit meekly and let Jan serve her lunch. And when it came to the point she was happy to see Jan and Frances stride off together and settle herself in the front parlour with the Sunday concert and her worries.

The doorbell startled her awake. Ringing for the second time? She rather thought so and hurried to answer it, feeling shaggy and demoralized with sleep.

'Sorry. I'm afraid I've wakened you.' Hugh stepped across the threshold. 'And sleep's what you need.'

'I seem to do nothing else.' She spared one quick glance at her dishevelled reflection in the hall mirror and led the way into the front room, turning off the radio as she went.

'Best thing you can do. You've a right to be tired. You've been under a lot of strain, you know, all winter, and now this.' He reached a professional hand to take her pulse and something very strange happened in her chest. 'Not too bad, considering.' He had noticed nothing. 'But I expected that, didn't bring my clobber.' He was, amazingly, without his black bag. 'You're a survivor; you'll cope.'

'I'm glad you think so.' It was suddenly the last straw to have him take it so completely for granted.

It got her a quick, sharp look. 'Have you cried?' he asked

'Cried? No. No, I haven't.'

172

'Well, it's time you did.' He reached into the pocket of his tweed jacket, produced a surprisingly clean white hand-kerchief and handed it to her.

'To order? Idiotic!' She began a laugh which turned into tears that grew into sobs.

'That's much better.' His firm arm settled her on the sofa and stayed around her shoulders. 'It's known as Brad-dock's crying cure and it works every time. Well, most times. Better than Valium any day.'

'I'm soaking your jacket.'

'What it's made for. Irish tweed.'

'It smells nice.' She blew her nose. 'I'm so ashamed. It's not Beatrice I'm crying for, or not only, it's for me too. I'm frightened, Hugh. I've got to start all over again and I'm not sure I'm up to it. Too tired. And I'm broke, too, would you believe it?' Suddenly it was all tumbling out – the cheques Beatrice wouldn't sign, her own dwindling bank balance and the letter from kind Mr Barnes telling her just how small her inheritance from her mother was going to be. 'I'm going to need a job fast, Hugh. Here, if possible; I'd like to stay. I know it seems heartless to be thinking like this, but do you know someone here in Leyning who might need me?'

'Yes,' said Hugh. '*I* do.'

She pulled away to sit up straight, dabbing her eyes with his sodden handkerchief. 'Oh, Hugh! I never thought. Your awful housekeeper! You'd fire her and let me take over? I could do that.' But could she? The idea was horrible.

'Oh, no you couldn't. Not like that. I'm not looking for a housekeeper, Helen, I'm looking for a wife.'

'Hugh!' She looked at him, thunderstruck.

'It's hopelessly the wrong moment, idiotically too soon, and all the wrong way round, but Helen, very dear Helen, it is what I have wanted to say to you since the first moment I saw you. Love at first sight. I didn't know it happened, certainly didn't think it happened to old codgers like me. Don't say anything yet, please.' He had felt her reaction. 'I know what a surprise, what a shock it must be to you. But think about it, please, dear, dearest Helen? Only first I must tell you the whole dismal lot, what I'm offering; so little. Sandra takes every penny she can get. You do know about Sandra?'

'Yes, someone told me; I'm sorry. But, surely, Hugh, she left you?' She seemed to have stopped crying.

'And had a child that could technically have been mine. And didn't marry the father. Which left me holding the baby. Or at least paying for it. And don't say I should have fought it; just think what that would have done to me here in Leyning. End of a career.'

'I'm afraid you're right. Imagine the Miss Fanshaws . . .'

'Exactly. But this is entirely the wrong conversation. What I'm trying to say is that I'm a poor man, Helen, always will be, but I'm a poor man who loves you. And needs you—'

'But I thought it was Frances—'

'Frances? So you've heard that story too! Trust Leyning. But, darling fool, surely even an innocent like you must know about Frances?'

'What do you mean?'

'She's gay. Always was, I suspect, but didn't know it. That's why we are such good friends now, she and I.'

'I see,' she said slowly. She was looking back over the winter, seeing so much, all of it in a new light. 'What an idiot I've been. But Hugh, Jan . . .'

'Probably,' he said. 'And none of your business. Our business, I hope. Helen, my only love, I am trying to ask you to marry me and you are making it remarkably difficult for me. All these red herrings!'

'Am I really that?' The world was reshaping itself around her.

'Difficult?'

'No.' She managed to say it: ' "Only love".'

'At first sight. So cross you were, going for me like an infuriated kitten.'

'You were so rude—'

'I was in such a hurry. I'm always in a hurry, Helen, always shall be, can't help it. And right now I'm in a furious hurry to cut free from Sandra and marry you, start our life together. And if you try to tell me you don't feel it too, I won't believe you. What happened when I took your pulse?'

'Something very strange.' Still safe in his arms she turned to look at him. 'You mean I've been in love with you all this time and didn't know it?'

'Didn't recognize the symptoms,' he said.

'I'd never had them before.'

'Good. No more had I, though I didn't realize it. Oh, my darling, we must be married just as soon as it's decent, not waste another minute. Beatrice would approve, I know she would. She teased me a little, you know, about coming to see her so often.'

'And I just thought the Leyning health service was wonderful.'

'Darling idiot.' He leaned towards her, and then, 'Hell and damnation!' They had both heard the sound of voices and a key in the lock. 'Are we going to tell them, Helen?'

'I don't see why not,' she said. 'Hugh, is it real? I'm not dreaming, am I?'

'If you are, we both are. And a very good dream too.' He

175

rose from beside her as Jan and Frances came into the room. 'Helen and I have a piece of good news for you,' he said. 'We are engaged to be married.'

'Oh, Helen!' said Jan.

And at the same moment: 'Hugh, Helen, I'm so pleased!' exclaimed Frances. 'It's almost too good to be true. I've been so worried; I just thought she was mad, been wondering how to tell you.'

'Tell us what?' asked Hugh. 'Who's mad, Frances? What are you talking about? Give it us straight. We can cope with anything now, can't we, Helen?'

'Absolutely anything.' Smiling at him.

Frances ran a hand through her short hair. 'It's worried me so much,' she told them. 'You remember, back after Christmas, when Beatrice summoned me to draft her will. I'd taken it for granted, you know, that it would either be all back to the family in America, or to some charity or other. Lots of lonely old ladies do that. Cats or dogs, that kind of thing. But not a bit of it. She had it all worked out. The house to you, Helen, and everything else to you, Hugh. And when I tried to tell her what a muddle that might create, she just said, "Nonsense, they are going to get married, those two", and nothing would shake her.'

'Well, I'll be damned. And, God bless her, she was absolutely right,' said Hugh. 'And I want it clearly understood that I am marrying you for the house, Helen.'

'Naturally,' she said. 'And I am marrying you for the money. What a good thing we didn't know. Oh, goodness!' It was sinking in. 'This lovely house, and all its memories. How lucky I am. . . . We are!'

'Luckier than you realize,' said Hugh. 'What a splendid woman, but what a fool. Do you realize, Helen, that if you had let her talk you into providing that cup of hemlock, there was your murder motive, staring the world in its face.'

'Ouch,' said Frances. 'And that goes for you too, Hugh.'

Jan was on her feet. 'I'm going to put some champagne in the fridge,' she told them. 'We've got some celebrating to do.'

'Yes,' Frances agreed. 'But before you do, Jan, one other thing. There's a legacy for Wendy of course, and one for you too, one I didn't understand. Paul's portrait by Vanessa Bell. Do you know about that, Helen?'

'Oh, yes, didn't I tell you? She keeps . . . she kept it in the closet in her room, said she couldn't face it any longer after she knew he wasn't coming back. Do fetch it, Jan. At the end of the closet.'

'No, let's take the champagne up to her room,' said Jan. 'Drink a toast to her there for the beloved witch she was.'

'Do let's,' said Helen as they all recognized this as a bridge to be crossed.

Beatrice's room looked very empty, but it smelled deliciously of the lily of the valley Helen had taken up as soon as the undertakers had gone the day before. By tacit consent they had filled their glasses downstairs; now she raised hers. 'To dear Beatrice.'

They drank it standing and Helen saw Jan close to tears. 'Fetch out the portrait, Jan dear,' she said. 'It's at the far end of the closet, tucked well away. I'd never have found it if Beatrice hadn't told me.'

'Right.' Jan put down her glass, opened the closet door and reached inside to produce the big canvas. She propped it on the chest of drawers, stepped back, and said, 'My God!'

It was Ben Norton who stared at them from the unfinished canvas, the fair hair, the blue eyes and the look that challenged the world.

177

'So that's why they left in such a hurry all those years ago after Benedicta's engagement party.' Helen had been working it out. 'Beatrice thought Paul and her sister were getting on too well by a half. She would never talk about that visit; I suppose she hoped she had got him away in time. The likeness must have skipped a generation, come out all too clear in Ben. No wonder his family didn't like him much, living proof of what they must always have suspected.'

'But Beatrice didn't see the likeness,' said Frances.

'You know how awful her sight was; she just saw people as blurs. And, remember, she did keep saying Ben reminded her of Paul.'

'So she did. And no wonder.'

'She couldn't see what colour his eyes were in the portrait,' Helen remembered. 'Asked me. Blue when he was happy, she told me, green when he lost his temper . . . What is it, Jan?'

'That's Ben,' said Jan. 'Night before last, his eyes went green. I was terrified.'

There was a little silence. Then, 'Dear Beatrice,' Helen said. 'I am so glad I didn't get her new glasses.' And got up to turn the picture to the wall. She did not want to think about Ben Norton.

The front doorbell rang.

'Damn,' said Jan, and went to answer it. She returned with Susan Fanshaw, looking distracted in a cardigan buttoned up wrong, wispy hair and no make-up.

'Oh, such a relief to see you go by.' She spoke to Frances as if there was no one else in the room. 'We saw you, Ellen and I, and she sent me straight away, while he's on the phone. He frightens us, rather. Oh, I should have said how sorry we are about poor Mrs Tresikker. I'm ashamed, but so much has happened since he came and told us. And I don't want to leave Ellen alone with him too long; it's when his eyes go funny, so scary, and what we need to know is how soon he can get his legacy and settle with the Black Swan, and, well, get away. Oh, thank you, Dr Braddock.' Hugh had put her gently into a chair and poured her a glass of champagne. 'How delicious. We really aren't used to having visitors, you see, only how could we turn him away when in a way we felt responsible for his being here at all. So, Frances dear, how soon . . . ?'

'I'm afraid it's bad news,' Frances told her. 'Mrs Tresikker only left Ben Norton her husband's papers and permission to publish them.'

'What? But he was so sure . . . Oh, my goodness me, what are we to do? He said it was just for the weekend, until he could get things worked out with Finch— With you people, Frances . . . Such a charming young man; we had no idea what it was really going to be like. So when we saw you going by, Ellen just told me to run for it. But what am I going to tell him?'

There was a little shocked silence as they took in the plight of the two old ladies saddled with this disastrous guest, so much more dangerous than they knew.

Jan spoke first. 'We've got to do something!' she said. 'Frances, think of something.'

'There's one thing we could do.' Frances spoke at last. 'Suppose we were to make him an offer for Paul Tresikker's papers? You've been working on them with Beatrice, Helen, haven't you? Mightn't you think of writing something about the two of them? Need the papers for that?'

'Oh?' Helen sounded as doubtful as she felt. She had other plans now.

'I could,' Jan broke in. 'I have to do a long paper next year. I could buy them. How much should I offer?'

'He hasn't even got a return ticket,' wailed Susan Fanshaw.

'Five hundred pounds,' said Frances. 'And I'll share it with you, Jan, or Finch & Finch will. We're partly responsible, after all. If James Finch hadn't let Miss Ellen persuade him to get in touch with the American lawyers, none of this would have happened.'

'But he had to do what we said, didn't he?' Miss Susan finished her champagne. 'Seeing as how we knew about him and Wendy. Mind you, now the little trollop has taken up with that dreadful black clergyman it'll all be different, won't it? You couldn't write me a cheque right now to take back with me, I suppose? He's pretty bored with being shut up in our house. I think he might just take it and go.'

'No,' said Frances.

'Yes,' said Jan.

'Hang on a minute.' Frances rose. 'I must make a call. Find Miss Susan something to eat, Helen?'

It was a long call, but Frances came back at last, looking relieved. 'Finch minimus is on his way,' she told them. 'He'll help if he can. He was in the office yesterday morning when Roger rang from the States about Ben Norton, as horrified as I was. He's about had it with his uncle and grandfather, didn't a bit like the way they let Miss Fanshaw talk them into alerting their American contacts about Mrs Tresikker, suggesting you were exerting undue influence, Helen. Sorry, Miss Susan, but there it is. Anyway, he feels responsible about it all and wants to help.'

Young John Finch arrived wonderfully soon. He looked very young indeed, but he was immensely helpful. He had brought five hundred pounds in cash, pointing out that a cheque would be useless to Ben Norton, and a carefully worded receipt for him to sign. Best of all, he volunteered to go back with Miss Susan and persuade Ben Norton to sign it. 'I'm afraid he would probably take it better from me,' he said with an apologetic glance at Frances.

'You are absolutely right,' she agreed cheerfully. 'And anyway, the less I see of that young man the happier I shall be. We think he shocked Mrs Tresikker on purpose.'

'Hoping to kill her?'

'And inherit. Yes. Use that, if he turns difficult.'

'I certainly will. Come along, Miss Susan, we've left your sister alone with that young man quite long enough.'

'Oh, thank you, Mr Finch. Such a comfort to have a man to cope with things.' She had eaten a sandwich, rebuttoned her cardigan and combed her hair, and went off almost cheerfully, still floating on her glass of champagne.

'Will it work, Frances, do you think?' Hugh asked.

'Oh, I think the combination of cash in hand and the judicious touch of blackmail will do it. He's a very capable fellow, that young John Finch, for all he looks about seventeen. He and I had quite a talk yesterday morning. We're thinking of starting up our own firm, he and I, and talking of blackmail, that bombshell of Miss Susan's about James Finch and Wendy may have given us just the lever we need to get John free of the two old barnacles he's been saddled with for so long. That really was a piece of news, and I'm sure it's true. Did you know, Hugh?'

'Oh, yes,' he said quietly. 'And the less said about it the better.'

'Of course.' She had the grace to look ashamed.

'And that goes for you too, Jan.' He turned to her. 'Not a word.'

'Not a word. But I hope it's true about Peter and Wendy.'

'If you want it to be, keep quiet. Leave them alone, don't even think about them.' He looked at his watch. 'Think about Helen and me instead. We have now been engaged for nearly two hours and we are overdue a little time alone. Why don't you two go and cook supper or something?'

'A very good idea,' said Frances. 'If you will stay for it? Come along, Jan, we know when we aren't wanted.'

'In Beatrice's room?' Jan looked at the two of them.

'She'd love it,' said Hugh. 'After all, she was the first to know, God bless her. What an amazing woman. Just think how she has changed all our lives. You and I are going to live here in her house, aren't we, Helen, and this is going to be our room. It's full of her still.'

'Not angry at all,' said Helen.

'Angry?'

'She called herself "angry old woman" in her advertisement. That's what brought me here. Caught my eye.'

'And she was, too,' said Jan. 'Do you remember, Helen—'

'You two are supposed to be cooking a celebration feast.' He turned to Helen as the door finally closed behind them. 'Now, my darling—' and his mobile rang in his pocket.